Death Life

Book 1

LEANNE VAN DONGEN

RoseDog❦Books
PITTSBURGH, PENNSYLVANIA 15238

RoseDog Books
585 Alpha Drive
Pittsburgh, PA 15238
Visit our website at *www.rosedogbookstore.com*

ISBN: 978-1-6470-2412-3
eISBN: 978-1-6470-2428-4

Also by Leanne Van Dongen:

The Showtime collection
Kate the Great
The Trio
Stage Fright

Prologue

She slowly opened her eyes to see the clear blue sky in front of her. Knowing perfectly well where she was, she sat up and gazed around; she was sitting on a field that seemed to be endless. She got to her feet, soft bright green grass tickling. Though she should have been sad that her time had come far too soon, she felt no emotions, unless feeling at peace counted.

A white stone staircase faded in from the blue sky. The bottom step was only a millimeter from her big toe. She looked to the top. Grey-and-white clouds were covering the sky, like icing spreading on a cake.

She placed her foot on the first step with a tap, and slowly ascended the stairs, never looking back. The skirt of her white dress bounced with each step climbing higher toward the clouds.

When she was close enough, she could see a golden archway—tiny as an ant—at the last step of the staircase. She knew exactly what her destination was. She ascended the stairs a little quicker, images of the one who would be waiting for her at the top filling her mind. Walking wasn't good enough; she began running and her speed increased due to having no lungs, no beating heart, and no cramping. Those days were behind her. Something brand new had occurred.

When she was close enough, she could make out the figure of a tall man in a white suit. He would be the first to greet her arrival.

At hearing range, the man called out, "Hello, Sweetie!"

She would have begun crying at the voice she hadn't heard in six years, but she also left her tears behind. The size of her father grew as she drew closer and closer.

And when she was right there, she threw herself at him, wrapping her arms around him and squeezing. He did the same, and they remained there for a long moment. She remembered what his hugs felt like and didn't want to break their embrace.

The sky returned to being blue and the rays of the white sun were upon them.

He sat on his knees—atop the cloud they stood on—and his pair of hazel eyes met the mini version.

"I missed you so much," said the girl. This would have been the moment to weep with absolute joy.

"I missed you, too," her father said back. "And you've grown."

In that moment, she realized other people—hundreds, maybe thousands—were watching them with joy; a daughter reuniting with her father.

But the tone changed when her father said, "Listen. Your time has come, but you're not ready to stay."

The girl frowned. "What do you mean? I'm here, aren't I?"

Her father sighed and put his hands on her shoulders, and would have been soothing her by rubbing gently with his thumbs if she was concerned. Again, no emotions. "You have to go back. Your sister needs you."

She sort of knew what he was referring to, but... "I can't. It's impossible. I wish I could help her—"

"That's what you're going to do: return to Earth and seek help. She needs a better life."

For the first time, the girl looked back at the staircase—still there when it should have disappeared by now. She turned back to her father. "What do I have to do?"

"Somehow find her help so she can start a new life."

"She doesn't even have one."

"Then help her get one. Do what you must. You're a smart girl and I believe you'll do the best thing to help her."

"When will I come back?"

"Once she's happy and has real friends."

"How long will it take?"

"That depends on you."

Her eyes looked down to the spot of grey beneath her feet. The touch of her father's fingers putting a strand of long blonde hair behind her ear made her look at him for the last time for a while.

"Go," he instructed. "I'll see you soon."

She gave him a final hug, turned away, and descended the white staircase, returning to Earth.

During the walk down, she thought hard about what she could do. But there wasn't much she *could do*...

It came to her: this wasn't something she could manage alone. She needed help from kind-hearted, intelligent people. She had to seek them out.

When she returned to Earth, she stopped to think. It wasn't the field she returned to, though. She was in a different location that didn't look like Ravendale. This place was too worn down. And before her was a prison, not like one you would see in Ravendale.

She didn't know what had brought her here, but she could have sworn she was in this location with the assistance of Heaven. Maybe God had put her here, and if He did, then what—who—she needed was around here somewhere...

Chapter 1

Felicity

I remembered that innocent girl I used to be; loved by many and rarely found in bad shit. I had so many wonderful friends. And Mom claimed I was the happiest girl in the world because I was always smiling. Even in the toughest of times, I wore a smile. But everything changed when Dad and I received news that Mom was killed in a car accident. I was twelve. By thirteen years old, my innocence was replaced with trouble. I lost myself over the one year after her passing. First, I quit doing the things I loved: mainly baking and ballet. Baking because it was something Mom and I had always done together, so to do that without her would have been heartbreaking. And ballet because Mom was the one who got me into ballet in the first place. She caught me secretly dancing to slow, peaceful music and suggested I do it. And I followed her idea, and loved it dearly. She watched me every time I went onstage and performed with other ballerinas. She put that love of ballet in my heart, so when her life came to an end, so did my passion for it.

Second, I changed my appearance. I began wearing clothing that was far from my normal style and wore dark makeup to help conceal my pain and help toughen me up, at the time. Then I got helix and lip piercing—I was getting to that.

Third, people who originally loved me despised the new Felicity Hale. The aftermath of my mother's death gave me a horrible reputation.

And fourth—the worst—I made new friends in high school who were terrible, and we got into a *lot* of bad shit. We got into trouble with the law for graffiti, robbing local stores, and—deeply regretted it immediately—drug abuse. That went back to lip piercing: when I was high one night, a thug attempted to rob me of my purse. I wasn't scared at first because my boyfriend and our troubled friends taught me combat skills, but what I didn't know was that the thug was armed with a knife and cut my lip on the right side, leaving an ugly scar. Dark lipstick and a lip ring hid it. But I did manage to knock the knife aside afterward and strike him directly in the face, knocking him out and leaving him on the sidewalk. One other incident that apparently happened when I was higher than the sky was that I attacked some woman and stole her purse, along with a lot of money. I had no memory of that event. I only knew of it because the cop who eventually found me and dragged me into custody informed me of what I'd done.

"Felicity."

I glared at a guard unlocking my cell door. "Time to go."

I rose from the bed and let him take me by the arm and lead me to where I would change into the clothes that I had arrived in. I went into the room and put on my white long-sleeved cropped shirt, ripped jeans, and white high-tops.

I had paperwork to fill out, and then I was released to go on with my shitty-as-hell life. Outside the prison, Dad's black truck was parked in a stall and I went to go greet him after two months, pushing back my long light blonde hair and shielding my eyes from the morning sun. When he saw me coming, his green eyes—my eyes—lit up. I opened the door and sat next to him, and he smiled like a clown. "Felicity, how are you?" he exclaimed.

"Shit," I responded honestly, in my dry voice. "Don't you think you should know that?"

Ignoring the question of disrespect, he leaned over and kissed my cheek. I just stared forward, gazing dumbly out the windshield.

Dad put his keys in the ignition and the engine rumbled. As he pulled out of the parking lot, he said, "So, I have something to tell you. And you have to listen." His voice lost its friendliness, not that I cared. I turned my head to look at him. "Last month, I moved into that house you and I were looking at. And you're going to a new school."

I did *not* like that. "But my friends—"

"Are not your friends anymore. You need real friends. Not a gang of losers."

2

"Thanks. I'm a member."

Dad shook his head at my comment.

I sighed. "I won't fit in."

"You will. I had a meeting with the principal, Mr. Wells, and he said the school community is great."

"Well, of course he's going to say that," I scoffed. "He has to."

Dad's eyes stared straight up—his way of showing irritation. "Try to work with me, City. Your loser-life is over. It's time for a new start. I want us to live normal lives like we used to."

Quietly and dryly, I said, "We can't. Not anymore. It's been like that for four years."

"We'll make it happen," Dad tried to assure me, though of course I had zero faith.

An hour passed on the road when Dad brought up, "I forgot to mention this: I told Principal Wells about your... conditions, and he recommended speaking to the school's counsellor."

"The school's counsellor? I don't want to. My issues are none of their business." I examined my plain nails. They had to be fixed. "Can you take me to the nail salon?"

After that, we continued on our adventure through the city of Ravendale to our new house, my thumbs, middle, and ring fingers red, my index fingers and pinkies glittery white with acrylics.

We pulled into the driveway of a brown and white, two story house. I stepped out of the truck and examined it. The place looked a little dull, but with flowers planted in the front yard, it would brighten up.

"Let's go inside!" Dad exclaimed and took the lead. The door opened smoothly and I peered around the place I only saw in pictures. There was a spiral staircase with white railings so shiny you could probably see your reflection in them. To the right was the living room and the laundry room was to the left.

"Look around," said Dad excitedly.

"What do you think I'm doing?".

"I mean go inside and explore."

I went in, not bothering to remove my high-tops. I slowly walked past the staircase, shoes tapping hard on the floor. The kitchen was rather big with a white marble counter and a glass kitchen table with two wooden chairs on opposite sides. The walls were a light shade of brown, when by the door the walls were white.

I glanced to the right to see that Dad had set up his office.

I went back to the stairs and ascended them to get an actual look of the upstairs. The walls were now beige. On the left side of the hallway were two bedrooms, one smaller than the other for some unknown reason, and the smaller one was mine. My stuff was in it, but packed in boxes. And on the right side was a large bathroom, the walls creamy yellow and decorated with sky blue tiles. It was pretty.

I went into my new bedroom—the walls white. My suitcase was resting on my ladybug-patterned duvet cover. My vanity, tall mirror, and dresser were against one wall and my desk, bookshelf, and closet across from them. Blue curtains blocked the sun's light as best they could.

I finished exploring my multi-coloured house and went back downstairs and checked out the massive backyard, squared in with the fence shared with three houses.

"What do you think?" Dad asked behind me.

"It's alright." I spun around to face him. "I have unpacking to do." I stalked past him and returned to my room. I unpacked everything. I put my clothes in the closet and dresser. My books, candles, a pink glass dove figurine, and framed pictures went on my shelf. My makeup was organized on my vanity.

Around ten, I wore a satin purple nightgown and sat on my bed with my back against the headboard, knees drawn up. I just sat in the dark and thought of how busy my day was and I had another busy one the next day with back-to-school shopping. Exhausted, I lay down and let my heavy eyes fall shut.

Chapter 2

Felicity

I awoke easily to my alarm clock, maybe because I was used to guards yelling me awake or inmates pounding on their cell doors in demand of breakfast.

I groaned, pissed off about my first day in a new school, and put on one of three outfits I put together for school: a purple long-sleeved cropped shirt with a knot, a denim vest with a red heart on the back, a denim skirt that was darker than the vest, a chain belt, and my white high-tops. I curled my hair and put it up in a ponytail. Then I decorated my face with red lipstick, mascara, black eyeshadow, and my lip ring. I always wore my diamond helix earrings. I lifted my purse from my desk chair and my binder from my desk.

I made my way to the nearest bus stop and waited to be picked up. Given how Mom was killed in a car crash, I became anxious about driving with Dad, so I bussed—though that wouldn't necessarily protect me from a fatal accident, but the risk wasn't as high. I stood there silently while a group of friends chatted and laughed away.

The bus showed up a couple of minutes later. I sat alone, and as the bus was delivering me to the new school, I studied the neighbourhoods we passed, trying to get a feel for my new home.

About ten minutes passed by the time it pulled up to a bus stop. Everyone unloaded themselves and, I guessed as a group, we walked the remaining five minutes to Ravendale Secondary.

It was a really big school with a billboard on the lawn reading "Welcome Back, Students." People were gathered all over the school grounds, no one standing alone, except me. I entered the school just as the bell sounded, and searched blindly in my purse for my schedule. I knew I found it when I felt a sharp cut on my finger, one only paper could make. I pulled it out and looked at it. I had English, biology, precalculus, and then chemistry. But all students had to report to their homerooms first, mine being my English class.

I found it by magically going down the right hallway, and walked in and found an empty desk. Students were pouring in, a lot of them noticing me, some looking longer than others, which I was used to, given how I was watched by dangerous inmates back in jail.

The second bell rang and the announcements came on. "Good morning, students," said a male voice, "and welcome back. We hope you had a wonderful summer."

Yeah. Wonderful.

I listened to what he had to say, not caring at all.

"Hello, everyone!" my English teacher, Ms. Donaldson, exclaimed. "So, all I'm going to do is give you your lockers. You can go find them and head to your first class." She was really nice.

"Felicity Hale?" she called when she reached my name on the attendance.

My hand rose.

"Your locker number is 624."

I brought my purse along for the helpless adventure of trying to find my locker. You would think it would be so easy to just look at other locker numbers and follow them.

"Do you need help, Miss?" a voice asked. I assumed it was for me. I whirled around to see a female teacher looking at me with question. "I'm looking for locker number 624."

"Follow me."

I trailed close behind as if I was a toddler chasing my mother all the way to the other side of the school. The teacher pointed at a locker within a long row of them. "Thank you so much," I said, but not in a kind way. Kindness was something I lacked a lot of.

But she didn't take it personally. "No problem."

I watched her go back in the route we came from and then opened my locker. There were two hooks, three shelves, and a mirror that was practically the back of the locker. I put my pad lock on it and returned to my English class.

The students were settled and Ms. Donaldson took the attendance intended for her English class. And she went on to talking about herself. She said she had been a teacher at Ravendale Secondary for two years. She blabbered on while I took in her appearance: golden blonde hair, hazel eyes, a lot of makeup, wore a white jean jacket over a blue and white striped dress and black heels, and really young. Early thirties?

We'd done literally nothing in the class. Maybe biology would be less boring.

I went in, and Mr. Wilson also introduced himself to his students, only this time we actually had something to do: form a study group. An issue—I didn't know anybody. Everybody managed to get into groups of three or four.

"Do you not have a group, Felicity?" Mr. Wilson asked.

Think really hard. I shook my head at the not-so-bright teacher.

"She can join us."

I turned my head back over my shoulder to see who the soft voice belonged to. Two girls were sitting in the back corner, one looking at Wilson, the other at me. I figured the voice belonged to the one staring at the teacher.

I took my purse and binder and joined them at the back.

"Perfect!" Wilson exclaimed. "Take a moment to introduce yourselves!"

The soft-voiced girl started with, "Hi, Felicity. I'm Janessa. Are you new here?"

I nodded, not returning her smile.

Janessa wore a burgundy cardigan with a black shirt underneath. On the chest was a bleeding heart. She had long light brown hair about the length mine was. Her lips were red, her eyes were brown, and her eyelids sparkly tan. She was beautiful.

"And I'm Allison," said the other girl, her voice thick. She wore a neon green T-shirt over a white long-sleeved shirt. Her warm red hair was short, and unlike me and Janessa, she wore zero makeup.

"It's nice to meet you both." Though it might not have sounded real, I meant it a hundred percent. I didn't know anyone. I may have just made two friends. But maybe I was pushing that theory. I just met them now. But I just wanted people to talk to here, and possibly make some friends if my personality didn't get in the way.

Chapter 3

Felicity

At lunch, I sat with Allison and Janessa at one of three empty tables in the cafeteria. So far, I was getting along with them, but only time would tell if that were to last. As I ate my pepperoni pizza, Janessa told me she was a figure skater, that she'd been doing it since she was six, and that she had a competition on Saturday. In some ways, I was a little upset to hear that she was doing an activity she loved whereas my love for ballet ended four years ago. I wasn't jealous, but my gut ached.

Allison didn't have much to say. Just that she and Janessa had been friends ever since kindergarten.

"What about you?" Janessa asked me, again with her smiles.

Well, my mother died when I was twelve, my life is shit, and I'm a former criminal.

"Tell us about yourself," Allison insisted when I stayed silent.

"Oh, excuse me, but could you skooch over to the floor?" asked the whiniest voice I ever heard.

The girls and I turned to a group of six people standing by our table. The girl who spoke had somewhat short and wavy dirty blonde hair. A boy a few inches taller than her stood at her side. And behind them were an Indian girl, a blue-haired boy, a girl with punk hair, and another girl who bared her braces. I turned back to Smiles and Allison, who wore looks of absolute unease. They glanced at each other and Allison began rising from her seat. Was she serious?

"Wait," I commanded.

Allison plopped back down and they both stared.

I turned back to the blonde ass. "I'm fine right where I am. Thanks." I didn't have an attitude, but I spoke with firmness.

It was as if the girl stopped breathing, she was so still. And her ass squad members looked at each other in shock. Blondie put her hands flat on the table and leaned down, staring at me as a pissed-off wolf would. "I said 'skooch.'" She even snarled like one. Was she trying to intimidate me? If anything, she was pissing *me* off.

"This is high school. Not a daycare for losers."

Once those words were spoken, a hush fell upon the whole cafeteria, and Smiles and Allison were staring down at the floor, frozen like ice.

Fire burned in the girl's eyes. But the guy next to her spoke the next set of words: "She sayed 'skooch.'"

My eyes narrowed on him suspiciously. "Sayed?"

The members encircled our table.

"What's your name?" Ass Leader hissed in my ear.

I turned my head slightly in her direction. "Felicity."

"Too long," she snapped. "What else?"

"Ummm… City?"

"City? More like Shitty."

Though it was weak, I smiled—something I seldom did anymore. And the girl wasn't pleased. She looked like she was ready to destroy me. "Are you new?"

"To this school and city."

"From what?" her assumed-boyfriend asked.

From where. "Who cares?" I spent four years of my non-innocent life in this kind of situation. I was used to people challenging me, but I never let them get away with it.

"Well," started Blue Boy, "we have to know as much as possible about our new enemy."

"Enemy?" I looked past Allison at him. "What the fuck is this?"

The Indian girl stood behind Janessa and stroked her scalp. "You're quite feisty, aren't you?" she asked me childishly.

Janessa jerked at the girl's touch and she looked to me for help, finally meeting my eyes again.

"Why so immature?" I scolded the group surrounding my friends and me, and glared.

Blondie snickered. "Alright, *Shitty*, I'll see you soon." She went to pat me on the head, but I snatched her wrist just above. I saw all this coming without having to think it through beforehand. I rose slowly from my chair, the tension of all sets of eyes of the viewers thickening, and looked her hard in the eyes. What I learned from my previous friends is you can't let assholes taunt you. Because once you've given them the desirable power, it could be a challenge to take it back. "I was wrong," I said calmly, but with a hint of hate, beginning to bend her wrist backwards, "I thought you were only assholes. You're psychopaths, too."

As Psycho Leader's wrist kept arching back, she grimaced. I continued to bend it to the point where if it were to go any farther, it would break, but I never broke the hold of our eye contact. And then I asked even calmer, "Are we going to have another problem?"

Her supposed boyfriend jumped to her rescue, seizing my wrist, forcing me to release Blondie's. "Let go," I warned, fingers curling into a fist.

He just hung on, his face unreadable.

The thing with me was that I only gave one warning for everyone who encountered a fight with me. Unfortunately for him, he didn't accept it. I brought my foot up and slammed it into his stomach. He stumbled back and fell on top of the table behind him. Everyone there backed away for safety reasons.

Blue Boy charged at me then, aiming to land a blow on my cheek. He threw his fist, but I caught it in my palm. My heart thundered like it did in every fight—from the adrenaline coursing through my body—as I hit him hard in the eye with my free hand. I let his fist go and watched him palm his eye. It would probably be blackened by tomorrow.

"Let's tell the principal," shrieked the girl with braces.

"No," Blue Boy grunted. "No. Let's just leave." He looked me dead in the eyes with his good one. "This ain't over."

I lifted my chin snootily only to trigger him.

The clan took off lightning-speed.

I settled my heart back to its normal pace and realized everyone was still watching, even when the excitement was over. "What?" I asked casually.

One by one, pairs of eyes drifted away from me and the cafeteria began to fill with chatter, slowly.

Janessa sighed with what I supposed was relief of nothing. "That was awesome."

I took my seat again. "What was awesome?" I glowered dryly.

"Do you know who they are?" Allison asked, leaning in. "Umm… you don't. The blonde girl's Maisie Clarke. She considers herself queen and the school her castle." She made a stupid smile at the idea of a psychopath calling herself queen, which I would have, too, if I wasn't still dumbstruck by all that had just happened. I simply raised my eyebrows.

"That guy who attacked you first—his name's Cody Parkson." Janessa took over. "Sometimes he says the wrong… never mind. The guy with blue hair is Will Peters. The girl with darker skin is Elaine Besak. The girl with punk hair is Daniella Hagen. And the girl with braces is Isla Lindberg."

"Is Cody Maisie's boyfriend?" I asked.

The girls nodded. "Everyone in the school knows who they are," Allison informed. "That group is hated and feared."

I shook my head at the stupidity of all these students. "This is too pathetic." I gaped at them, not believing this. In what high school did *this* happen? Even Thumber didn't have issues like this. I totally understood why the Ass Squad was hated. It was all in the name. But why feared? There was nothing to be afraid of. Just stand up for yourself and report this to a staff or someone who could take care of it.

Sadness developed in Allison's eyes. Turning to Janessa, she asked quietly, "Do you think she's gotten worse since Amber died?"

Janessa's eyes were coated with sorrow then.

I looked between them. "Amber?"

Their eyes settled on me. "Amber Clarke," they said, voices overlapping.

I digested it for a second. "Maisie's sister?"

"Younger sister," Janessa specified. "Amber drowned in their pool in the summer."

Even though I despised Maisie, my heart sank a couple of inches. "Oh, my god."

The girls nodded slowly. "She was twelve."

"Sad," I remarked with meaning, but dryly. I didn't show them much, but I still had minor feelings. They weren't noticeable with my dry way of talking and way of looking at people.

Janessa said quietly, "I couldn't imagine losing my brothers."

"I couldn't imagine losing Joy," Allison added.

I knew exactly what it was like to lose a loved one.

My next class was precalculus. And something about the teacher made me dislike him very much in one glance. I was about to find out what it was. Mr. Wagner was really tall, had grey hair, and had dark eyes.

I took my seat near one of his two desks, and when the second bell rang, he walked from his desk to the front of the room. "Hello, I'm Mr. Wagner," he started in a very thick German accent. "I've been teaching at Ravendale Secondary School for thirty years. I grew up in Germany."

Can you please go back?

The subject suddenly changed. "You all need a workbook by next class. With me, you'll be getting homework every day, and it's worth ten percent of your mark. Quizzes are twenty. Tests are seventy."

I felt my eyes widen. *Holy damn.*

He then blabbered on about nonimportant things.

After half an hour of useless talk, he gave us a quiz on what we learned in precalculus 11, which I didn't like at all because I needed time to study for tests and quizzes.

And, of course, I screwed up bad and knew I failed miserably. I didn't need to see the mark to know. I had common sense to tell me.

For the duration of the class, I was noticing how the other students looked at him: fear and despite coloured their eyes. But why were they scared? Wagner was a joke.

Class ended ten minutes after everyone had finished the quiz, and as I was walking out the door, I felt his smile, but I didn't repay it.

Chemistry was going way better. Mrs. Kravets was also really nice and cheery. Like the other teachers, she talked about herself and discussed how great the school community was. But I thought she was dead wrong.

My first day of school could have been better, but oh well.

As Dad and I had dinner, I told him about my crappy day. He felt bad about all I said, and agreed there shouldn't be fights over a lunch table, that it was beyond pathetic. "It's not daycare" he had said. My words exactly.

Around ten, I was ready for bed and quickly ran a comb through my tangled hair in front of my vanity mirror.

"Felicity."

My mind was elsewhere when I heard my name. "Yeah?" I asked, turning my head to the door, expecting to see Dad. But the doorframe was empty.

13

"Felicity." This time, it was like wispy singing.

I stopped combing my hair and just listened and examined my room—only furniture and soundless. I felt a bit of concern of hearing my name for the possibly third time. It never came back.

Chapter 4

Janessa

I had my alarm set for seven, but automatically woke up at six-thirty. I lay on my bed and stared up at the ceiling, thinking about what happened between Felicity and Maisie. I was so sure Felicity was making a huge error of challenging Maisie when Maisie originally challenged her. But she totally stood her ground and didn't let herself be victimized, like most people in Ravendale Secondary did. The entire school feared Maisie and her squad. But Felicity—she was fearless... and she didn't seem to be the friendly type to begin with. All the dark makeup and piercing... her way of looking at you... her way of talking to you... Honestly, I was a little afraid of her at first, but I got used to it in just over an hour. Even though she wasn't friendly, she was actually really cool.

The flashbacks dispersed like mist and I got dressed. I put on a black long-sleeved shirt with pink varsity stripes, black leggings, and a white skirt overtop. I braided two strands of my light brown hair and tied them together behind my neck with a tiny elastic. I applied light brown eyeshadow and pale pink lip gloss.

"JANESSA!" my youngest brother Caleb boomed from the other side of the door. "BREAKFAST!" He was quite the screamer, which, I guessed, was typical for six-year-old boys. My other brothers Alexander (Alex), Lukas (Luke), and Lee, and I thought it super irritating, but we loved it at the same time.

"JANESSA?! ARE YOU COMING?!"

"Yeah!"

"OKAY!"

I crossed my enormous room to the door and walked down a white hallway with golden swirls patterned on the walls, framed pictures scattered.

I descended fancy white marble stairs with gold wavy railings and stepped onto the balcony and descended one of two larger versions of the stairs to the pale brown floor. I went left to the dining room, the family's two German shepherds Dorothy and Belle greeting me with heavy panting and slapping tails. I named them after two characters from my favourite childhood movies *The Wizard of Oz* and *Beauty and the Beast*. My parents got them when I was nine.

"Hey," I cooed, rubbing their fuzzy heads. I sat with my brothers, who were still in their pajamas, at the end of the table and Kira—one of three maids—stood at my side and put cereal in my bowl. "Thanks."

"You're welcome."

When you had a father who acted and a mother who sang, you were mostly looked after by people who were paid to replace the parents. Sometimes my brothers and I missed them, but we were fine.

I shoved a spoonful of cereal into my mouth and looked up at the chandelier, glistening above the glass table. Its light reflected on the glass. I then eyed the giant painting on the wall. It was of a woman wearing a princess-like gown and sleeping on a bed of roses. Paintings and pictures were scattered throughout the mansion.

At eight, Denise, another maid, had Caleb, Luke, and Lee in her car and Alex and I hopped into my blue Honda Accord. Alex was changed into a black hoodie with a skull on the back that had blood running down from the eye sockets, ripped jeans, and Nike shoes. His light brown hair was nicely combed, his bangs swept to the left and covering his eyebrow.

As we drove, he said, "I saw what happened with your friend yesterday."

I managed a quick glance at him. "I'm sure everyone did. Nobody has ever stood up to Maisie before. It's crazy."

"Who is she actually?"

"Her name's Felicity. She's new in town."

"She's kind of hot," he said casually. "Such a badass."

Disturbed, I rolled my eyes.

"What else do you know about her?" he pressed.

16

This conversation was the weirdest one I'd ever been involved in, but I played along as if it was totally normal. "Actually, not much. Allison and I asked her about herself, but she wouldn't say anything. It's like she's secretive."

"Maybe she is."

The conversation fell silent and I loved the sound of it.

"*Is* she your friend?"

Wow. The boy fell in love at first sight. But with the wrong person.

My answer was hesitant. "I… think so. She seems cool."

"Is she nice?"

"Nice, but lacks friendliness. Just to put it out there, I haven't seen her smile."

"She doesn't seem the smiley type."

"She doesn't seem happy. It's as if something is *seriously* wrong."

Alex patted my knee and said in his happy voice, "You'll find out."

We arrived at school and I parked. We told each other to have a good day. My first class was precalculus.

And I was a little scared when I laid eyes on Mr. Wagner. I didn't fully study him, but that one glance said…

He started class by talking about what we needed to know about him, and then went on to discussing unrelated things. I thought it was fine. Then he gave us a quiz! It was based on what we learned in the previous year of precalculus. That was an issue, because for me, when I didn't practice math repetitively, I would forget everything, and I would have to relearn it all. In my opinion, I didn't think it was fair to give quizzes for the first class.

I "finished" the quiz and handed it in, knowing how "well" I did. *That* I didn't like about him, but I wasn't ready to dislike him yet. I guessed that was pretty obvious given how it was only day one. I tried to like all of my teachers as much as possible. I thought it was better that way, to get along with them so the school year went smoother.

My next class was PE. I changed into my PE strip and put my hair up in a ponytail and entered the gym with the rest of my classmates.

Ms. Moretti wore all black and had reddish hair. We played ball hockey, which I loved. And I really liked her enthusiasm when I got two goals.

And then lunch came. I wasn't looking forward to it. But Felicity being smart like she was thought we should sit around the corner in the cafeteria to avoid the most malicious people in the school. She, Allison, and I were hidden from eighty percent of the students. And it was working. We ate and talked in peace.

Allison and Felicity were talking away when Alex's question popped into my head: *What else do you know about her?*

"Where did you come from?" I asked a question very much unrelated to their discussion. They looked at me with confusion, but I pushed the embarrassment aside. "What city, I mean."

"Thumber," Felicity answered dryly. Her voice was always dry it seemed.

"Why did you move?"

She only stared. *Strange.*

Allison looked between us, silently agreeing the silence awkward.

"Um," Felicity finally said, "my dad got a new job."

I nodded and raised my eyebrows. Why did it take so long to answer a simple question with a simple answer?

Allison continued to glance between us.

"What class do you have next?" Felicity asked us, clearly wanting to talk about something else.

I scavenged through my small backpack for my schedule. "English," I replied once I found it. "With Ms. Donaldson."

"She's really nice," Allison informed me.

Felicity nodded in agreement. "A hell of a lot better than Wagner."

"Oh, my god," I breathed. "I'm kind of scared of him."

Felicity shrugged. Of course *she* wasn't.

Well, the rest of my day should have been better.

Chapter 5

Janessa

Sitting on the bench by the boards, I waited for two minutes to pass. I sat upon my gloved hands, trying to keep them warm. Ravendale Arena was frigid, and a few of the skaters complained over it.

"Hi."

Carly came towards me, skate guards clicking with each step.

"Hey," I returned. "How was school?"

"Pretty good. How 'bout you?"

"It was alright."

"Glad to be back?"

"Hell no."

"I am."

I gave her a weird-friendly smile. "How do you like school?"

"Just do. No reason."

The rest of the skaters joined us by the boards. Maggie smiled nicely. Sammie and Dessa said, "Hello." Jessica waved; she wasn't much of a talker. And Lynn, Charlette, and Annabelle (Anne) had a conversation going, so they didn't notice us around them.

When a couple of minutes passed, the nine of us stepped onto the ice to warm up.

We completed a lap before turning backwards.

And no one had finished warming up when Melinda shouted, "Okay!" It echoed across the ice. She skated to the end-line. "Line up for…" I didn't hear the rest.

On the end-line, Melinda divided us into three lines. "We're just going to do spins today," she said. Melinda played slow-paced music. "Sit spin."

Maggie, Carly, and I were first. We skated a little ways up, turned backwards, and went down on one leg, the other stretched out before us.

The next set went, pushing me, Maggie, and Carly up to the next line.

When us three made it to the end, we went back to the beginning alongside the boards.

"Camel sit," Melinda said.

Group development was for thirty minutes, and then it was free skate. Carly and I watched each other do jumps and spins and made judgements on how to improve them.

Carly took off poorly into an axel, her skates not lifting off the ice high enough, and she didn't complete a full rotation. "You're leaning forward too much," I coached. "Let me show you." I skated to the center of the ice and skated backwards around the circle before turning forward, drawing my arms back, and taking the leap. I came back to her. "That was good," she complimented.

"Try again."

After ten minutes, Melinda came up to us and said to me, "Let's do a run-through of your solo."

The *one* important thing I should have been working on I forgot to work on. The competition was on Saturday.

Carly skated off on her own while I took my position at center ice. My arms were above my head ballet-like and I waited for my piece of ballet music. When it echoed across the ice, I gracefully lowered my right arm, watching it descend to my waist and my hand curving as if I was cupping something inside. I mirrored that with my left arm. Keeping my hands still, I twirled on my toe picks like a ballerina, and my arms ascended as I spun backwards and skated in a circle, picking up speed, and took off into an axel in time to the sudden boom of the dramatic moment of the music. The calm of the ballet ended and the drama controlled my leaps and turns and spins and jumps, keeping me quick on my skates. I spun in a layback spin, hands high above my head, the world spinning around and around upside down. Coming out of the spin, the world turned right-side up. I skated around the edge of the boards, gaining the speed

I required, and lifted my right leg into a spiral, my blade way higher than my head, gliding until forever before letting it drop gracefully.

The music slowed and the peacefulness of the music returned to die once again. I did little ballerina moves before coming to the end of my solo, arms in an X across my chest and my right leg crossed behind my left, toe pick dug into the ice.

I breathed deeply and glided toward Melinda. "That was good." She grinned and asked, "Do you have your dress?"

"It'll be ready."

"Makeup decided? Hair?"

I nodded.

"Alright. Keep practicing."

"Okay."

Melinda smiled before moving on to the next skater, and I skated with Carly for the remainder of the session, performing our solos for each other a couple of times.

"So, how was everyone's day?" Denise asked during dinner.

All eyes locked on me since I was always the first to talk. "School and skating were fine."

"I had a science test," Luke spoke next. "It was really easy." Science was his favourite class and the only one in which he received an A on every assignment, project, quiz, and test.

Lee was next in line. "School was alright."

"I got in a fight," Alex said.

"Did you win?" Caleb asked, excitement all over his face. For whatever reason, he got intrigued by hearing our brothers' stories of their brawls, which wasn't very good.

"Oh, yeah. So, this guy in PE picked a fight with me for accidently kicking a soccer ball at his head. A few guys and I tried explaining it was an accident, but he wouldn't listen."

"What did you do to him?" Lee asked from across the table.

"Just swung him around by the arm until his legs gave out and I got on top of him and blew his lip up."

Denise stared.

"Blew his lip up?" Caleb asked, confused.

"It means he punched his lip so hard it burst with blood," Luke explained. "Ouch."

"Are you suspended?" I asked Alex from beside him.

"No. The teacher left for a moment and that was when it all happened."

"Wouldn't he snitch on you?" Lee asked.

"He's not a snitch."

"You better hope he's not," said Caleb. "Anyway, I painted a picture of an apple tree."

I had a bath, slipped on a light purple satin pajama top and minty green furry pajama pants. I always mixed up my pajamas. I blow-dried my hair and headed to bed. Malia—the third maid—asked if I needed anything before leaving me solo in my massive, dark room, the only light coming from my phone as I set my alarm.

Knock, knock.

The door opened and I turned on my phone's flashlight and shined it on the person entering—Alex. "What?" I asked with a yawn, turning the flashlight off.

He crossed half the room before taking a seat on the bedside, a hand on my knee. "Any more info on Felicity?"

I thought for a moment, staring dumbly at him. "She moved from Thumber."

He waited for more, looking intently.

"Because her dad got a new job."

He wanted more. Something that would interest him. But I had nothing. "Anything else?"

I shook my head, and since our eyes adjusted to the dark, he saw it and sighed with disappointment, removed his hand from my knee, and went to the door.

"It was strange, though."

My sudden words made him stop and turn. He came to stand next to me, but while his eyes were on me, mine were on the ceiling as I recalled Felicity's behaviour today at school. "I asked Felicity why she moved here and she didn't answer right away." My eyes flicked to Alex's. "It took a moment for her to reply 'my dad got a new job.' And then she immediately changed the topic."

"So, she *is* secretive," he observed, agreeing with the description I gave him of her earlier today.

"Something's up, and she won't talk about it."

"Give it some time. She'll open up when she's ready."

I nodded and shifted my eyes down on my hands, folded on my stomach. "Yeah, you're right."

Alex was leaving again. "Good night," I heard him say.

"Good night."

The door shut.

Lying awake, I thought of how weird Felicity was being—

The beginning of my thoughts was interrupted by the sudden agonizing pain I felt within. It was as if someone was crushing my heart. Literally. I sat up fast and clutched my stomach and chest and breathed heavily and whined over the pain. And then I felt something tickling my lip and going down my chin. I threw the duvet cover off me and ran to turn the light on and looked in the mirror; it was blood! It dripped off my chin, drop after drop. The amount of it increased and gushed out of my mouth and onto my pajamas like a waterfall running down a mountain, and the pain was sharper. I released a scream and cried wildly as I fell onto my back, still clutching my chest and stomach.

My brothers and maids stormed into my room and rushed to my sides, but that didn't ease the screaming and wailing. "I'm calling 911!" Denise panicked, bolting back out.

Alex lifted my upper body onto his lap and cupped my bloodied face and Luke and Lee held my hands tight. They were just as horrified as I was. Caleb collapsed to his knees and wept, traumatized by the scene.

Blood and screams continued to flow out of my mouth, and Alex and I were caked in my blood.

"It's going to be okay!" he screamed over mine and Caleb's wailing. Tears sprung to all of our eyes.

I lost more and more blood by the second and now my brothers and I were in a pond of crimson. Kira and Malia backed away from the pond growing in size, just watching the horror of it all, frightened for my life source pouring out.

It was when the paramedics arrived that the blood rush and pain just... vanished. It was too weird to make any sense of it. It just... stopped?

Chapter 6

Allison

Joy shook me around violently as if she was trying to determine whether I was dead or not, until my eyes opened. "Al-son," she stuttered.

I sat up in bed. "What are you doing?" I asked sweetly. I was trying to see her through the blackness of our room.

"I h-had a ni-nightmare."

I blindly searched for her hand, and when I found the roughness of chipped nail polish, I squeezed the hand the nails belonged to. "It's alright," I soothed. "Go back to sleep."

"Dad was i-in it."

I stared at the dark. It enraged me how Dad ditched me, Joy, and Mom. I remembered how I loved him once. Now I wished death upon him. "Don't be upset, Joy," I encouraged, though she had every right to be pissed. "Mom and I are here." Our hands broke apart and I heard metal squeaking as Joy climbed the ladder to her bunk.

I lay back down, eyes wide open. I was a happy girl, but at times life was hard. I had loving parents and lived in a nice house once. Dad adored me, Joy, and Mom so much that I would have thought he would never have had abandoned us. He took us on really nice vacations, taught me how to ride a skateboard, took us to see a movie twice a month… everything. But the good times turned bad when I was thirteen. Joy's elementary school teacher noticed something strange in her behaviour and requested a meeting with our parents. One thing Joy did was pretend to be asleep to annoy her. And there was something else, something my parents and I already noticed, but didn't give much thought into: she stuttered. She had difficulty forming words properly. My parents took Joy to see a doctor and learned that she was mentally challenged. My parents and I were shocked by the news, Dad being shocked the most. I was pretty sure he tried to cope with having a disabled child, but the dread was too much to bear, so… Mom, Joy, and I were basically ordered to move out by him—in words that implied it. We packed our belongings and Mom took twenty thousand dollars from the safe. We temporarily lived with Mom's sister for two years. During that time, Mom earned enough money for a rather big apartment in downtown Ravendale. So, we lived here for two years. Joy had nightmares of our father for four years. She felt ashamed of herself and blamed herself for his rejection. I had nightmares, too, but when I was able to handle the fact that he did this to us, I hadn't had them for about a year now. I had to learn that you had to accept the past for what it was in order to live on.

That four-year journey was very stressful and scary. I would never forgive Dad for how he treated us, especially his ten-year-old daughter.

The traumatizing memories of the past four years made tears fall down my temples.

I wept until the room lightened with the emerging dawn. It was almost six and my sister and I woke at six-thirty on school days. Ravendale Secondary was uptown, so I needed to leave early.

I went to the window wall and pushed the burgundy curtains aside. I slid the glass door open and stepped onto the balcony. The wind blew through my short hair and black nightgown. I sat on the railing, facing out to the yellowing of the sky, but a skyscraper hid the sun. My feet rested on a platform, high above the early-morning traffic.

This was my favourite spot to be. I found it soothing, especially with the wind.

It felt exactly like half an hour when Joy came out. "Al-son?"

I swung back over the rail and got ready for school, putting on a shirt underneath a jean jacket, white pants, and a hairband. I went to the kitchen. Mom was sipping coffee from her polka-dotted cup, and she wore her housecoat. "I'll have a cup." I didn't drink coffee often. I sat at the table as she poured me a cup and placed it down in front of me. "Joy had another nightmare," I told her.

She sighed. "Maybe I should get her help."

I shrugged. "Maybe."

In that moment, Joy joined me at the table, wearing a black T-shirt with the Batman symbol on the chest, blue leggings, and a wristband. Her long warm red hair was in pigtails. Mom gave her pink lemonade.

Joy and Janessa's youngest brother Caleb were total superhero fans. Every Halloween, they dressed up as the male and female version of a superhero and went trick-or-treating together. They were very close, like Janessa and I were. All of Janessa's brothers loved Joy, but Caleb adored her the most. *They* were like siblings. Joy saw him grow up to six years old. She had always been in his life. But he missed out on the first four years of hers.

After breakfast, Mom drove Joy to school and I took the sky train, my transport to uptown Ravendale and back. It took about forty-five minutes to get there, but it never bothered me. I actually enjoyed taking the sky train and viewing the city from above.

Chapter 7

Allison

"Is Janessa not here yet?" I asked Felicity as I took my seat next to her.

"I haven't seen her." Her voice was dry—as always—and she looked at me darkly, her way of looking at people. I was rather shaken by her; she had a dark personality, it seemed like.

Class started.

"So, I know this is only your second class with me," Mr. Wilson started, "but I'm assigning you a mini project."

"Oh, *what*?!" two boys called out angrily. But Mr. Wilson didn't care. "With your study group, you're going to make a presentation on safety in the classroom, identifying the safety equipment and where they're located in the room. You've learned this before, so it shouldn't be hard. You have this block to plan everything out. It's due next class."

No one moved at first, dazed by the way-too-early-assigned project. Except me. Being a school-lover, I got right into with the dazed Felicity. "We can start without Janessa."

Everyone got to work as if "we can start without Janessa" was the signal to go.

"How do you want to do it?"

"We could make a PowerPoint," Felicity suggested. "Like, draw a map of the room, take a picture of it, and put it on a slide."

"If *I* do that, could you and Janessa maybe make the presentation and list the rules?"

The thing I couldn't figure out about her was how she thought of people and their decisions; she gave no clue with her face. Just the answer using her mouth. "We have to do it together."

There we go.

"But whatever," she decided just then, not... giving... a... damn... anymore? "I just don't understand why you only make the map and Janessa and I do everything else."

I had to give up the truth. I met her two days ago and she had to know about my sister. Too soon. "It's just that..." it was hard to say... "My sister needs quite a bit of extra care."

"Extra care," she repeated flatly. She watched me curiously, and I guessed her eyes wanted a better explanation. "My sister is... mentally challenged, and she hasn't been doing well for years."

I might have been mistaken—very likely—but I was pretty sure an emotional soft touch coated her eyes. Did she really feel emotions other than anger?

Abandoning the conversation in hopes I explained enough, I went to the front of the class for a blank sheet of paper. I turned back around to see Tristan looking past his friend at her. But Felicity didn't notice, her green eyes fixated on me. She realized I was glancing between her and someone else, so her eyes flicked to where mine were. Tristan looked away sheepishly.

I placed myself back beside Felicity and took my ruler out from my binder and created a border around the sheet.

"Tell me about your sister."

Her eyes might have softened a teeny-weeny bit, but her voice remained as dry as the desert.

"Her name's Joy," I said. "She's ten."

And the silence that followed bothered her. It was clear as a crystal. "What else?"

I slowly lifted my eyes from the paper and gazed forward, debating whether it was her business to know about Joy's conditions or not. Maybe it wasn't time yet. But the pressure of her eyes was intimidating. But it wasn't like she was going to attack me for it.

"Do you not want to talk about it?"

My eyes shifted to Felicity and I gave in to her curious stare. Her lips parted. There was a gap that was the size of a fly.

I guessed she could know about my past. I felt it was too soon, but whatever. Uncomfortably, I said, "My parents and I found out that Joy is mentally challenged when she was six, and her grade one teacher brought to our attention that her behavior was strange."

If I was right about Felicity's eyes softening, they didn't soften any more than they already had.

"She doesn't *always* stutter, though," I continued, shoulders shifting uneasily. "Sometimes she can properly form a word or two, but then she'll stutter on the next and possibly the one after. And because of another issue, she needs quite a bit of attention. It would be great if you and Janessa could make the presentation so that I have more time for Joy."

As fast as light, her eyes flicked down and flicked back up. *That* I knew I saw. If I was correct about her lightening eyes, then she was definitely not one for exposing her emotions much. Which *did* make sense; the way she looked at you, the way she talked to you…

"Is she a happy girl?"

What the hell? "Well, I think she tries to be happy…" A smile tugged at the corners of my mouth, but in a not-so-happy way. "She's a great sister… but it's been hard for her to be happy ever since…"

"What?"

I brushed it off by turning back to the map I had to draw. "So, you don't mind putting the presentation together with Janessa?"

There was a short pause of stupidity; Felicity wasn't an idiot. She knew I purposely rejected her want of me to get into the dark past Joy, Mom, and I lived together. But that was for another time, and she respected that. "Yeah, that's fine."

"Okay, cool."

My next class was physics with Mr. Caprenter. My favourite class with my favourite teacher. Plus my boyfriend Roman Jashari and our friend Yūki Ito. Roman and I had been a couple, and friends with Yūki, for a year. Yūki was from Japan.

I joined them at the back of the room, but didn't realize my approach until I lay a hand on Roman's head, his black gelled hair pricking my fingers. He wore a black and blue plaid jacket, ripped jeans, and white Vans.

And Yūki was wearing a jean jacket, grey sweat pants, and black Nike Dunks. He had an emo hairstyle, dyed with a little blond.

I sat next to Roman and he wrapped his arm around my shoulders and I leaned against him. But his attention wasn't ready for me yet.

Mr. Carpenter walked into the room at the same time the bell rang. "How's everyone?" he asked cheerfully.

No one had anything to say, but a few heads nodded.

"I can already tell this will be my quiet class. Today we're just going to do a review from the textbook, pages..." He flipped through his binder lying on his desk... "twenty to twenty-four, questions one to nine, thirteen to twenty-three, twenty-five to thirty, and thirty-four."

"Will you be kind enough to get me a textbook?" I asked Roman childishly as I lifted off his shoulder.

"Alright." He joined the pack of students grabbing very thick textbooks from the shelf.

"And me!" Yūki called after him. Though he was from Japan, his accent sounded a little North American.

Roman returned with three, and tipped the pile over to let the top slide off in front of me. "Thank you," I sang like a child.

Yūki took the next one on top. "Thanks."

I flipped to page twenty and took a blank sheet of paper out of my binder. The first section of the review was based on temperature and calorimeter. Question one read "A car travels at 270 km in 9 hrs. What is the average speed for the trip in km/h?" and the answer "30 km/h." was my answer.

Next question: Convert minus thirteen degrees Celsius to Kelvin.
Answer: 260.15K.

Question: What is the primary heating method you experience when you are sitting around a camp fire?
Answer: Radiation.

I got the answers except for nine. "Hey, Roman?" I asked in my normal voice.
"One moment... Yeah?"
"What did you get for nine?"
"Infrared is lower frequency than ultraviolet."
"Thanks."

The review was completed by the end of the class.

Felicity and I sat together at lunch.

English was my next class—didn't do much.

And sociology was last. We began Unit 1, the introduction to sociology. We were going to learn about the discipline in sociology, how sociology developed as a field of research, and study various central theoretical perspectives. It sounded really interesting and difficult, but every course I was taking was on the harder side.

Chapter 8

Allison

I gently ran Joy's hairbrush through her hair, a deeper shade of red due to just being in the shower. "What was your favourite part of school today?" I asked sweetly. That was our evening thing; after our showers, we would brush each other's hair and talk about our favourite part of school that day. On weekends, we talked about our favourite part of the day. It was something Joy decided to do long ago.

"Mmmmm… proba-bly art because I-I ma-made a painting."

"What did you paint?"

"An ocean."

"You have to bring it home and show me."

"Yes, I do." There was excitement in her voice. She was always excited about showing me and Mom things she had made.

I stopped brushing, the bathroom light making her sleek and wet hair shine gold in some areas. It was her turn to brush mine. Putting her brush back in the drawer, Joy brought mine out. I put my back to her and sat cross-legged on the mother of pearl tiles.

After three brushstrokes, she asked, "What w-was your fav-our-ite part of school to-day?"

"Um…" I thought hard. "Physics."

"Why physics?"

"Because we did a review and it was fun and easy."

Each brushstroke was slow and satisfying and my eyes shut.

"All done."

My eyes opened.

"It doesn't ta-take long t-to brush your ha-ir be-because it's short," she said matter-of-factly, "not long like mi-mine."

"Yeah, you have long, beautiful hair." I looked back at her over a shoulder. She was beaming at the compliment and put my hairbrush back in the drawer. We walked to the living room, her leading me by the wrist, and we watched cartoons until nine-thirty.

"Good night," we said to Mom.

She returned it.

Joy climbed the squeaking ladder to the top bunk and I snuggled into the duvet cover below. And just as my eyes were beginning to close, I caught a glimpse of what seemed to be a silhouette of a girl standing perfectly still in the middle of the room. Assuming it was just tiredness, I let my eyes fall shut and drifted off.

I strolled down the middle of a street in an area I didn't recognize. There were houses, but I appeared to be completely alone. The area was dead. I stopped in my tracks and had a good look around, trying to get some sort of feel of my location.

I continued on to an unknown place my feet decided to take me. I turned a corner and travelled down the apparent-endless road; far down, I couldn't see anything. But my destination awaited me down there, according to my legs. There were no houses. Just… nothing. Literally nothing.

I looked back at the houses shrinking with distance.

When I turned forward, my feet stopped, telling me the journey had come to an end. Before me was a run-down house—it wasn't there before—in the center of a group of dead trees on either side. It looked as if it had been abandoned—

Like a snap of fingers, day turned to night, and light shined through the windows, giving the house back a touch of life that might have been stolen—

Then there was a scream.

My eyes flared opened with a start and I sat up. It had all been a dream. Possibly the weirdest of mine.

Shaking my head, I looked to the spot where I thought I saw a shadowed girl and it was still there. I peered hard through the dark of the room and *actually* saw someone, or something. Inner screams were collecting into a bundle. Then came a wispy giggle, which at first I thought belonged to Joy, but her giggles didn't sound like that. The shadowed girl made them I realized a second later. I set my bundle of screams free.

"What?! What?!" Joy yelled in a terrified manner.

A rush of footsteps from the hallway followed, growing in sound. Mom threw open the door and flicked the light switch on. "What?! What's wrong?!"

I looked to her, expecting her to be looking directly at the intruder. Not me. My eyes went back to where the shadowed girl was... The girl wasn't there. How could she have just vanished in the time it took for my eyes to leave her briefly for Mom and then back at her?

The screams had taken all my energy and I was breathing like I was dying. "Something... was there."

Metal squeaked. "There's noth-nothing here," Joy observed. She and Mom sat on either side of me, trying to give me comfort. They were concerned as hell. "There was," I managed a little more normally. "It was... laughing or something."

Mom frowned. "I think you had a nightmare."

"It wasn't a nightmare," I whined for belief.

We went quiet as I examined the room for the intruder.

"I don't know, Allison," Mom said shakily.

Breathing turned easier. "Neither do I." If there really was nothing there, then that was a dream, but what about the giggles in reality?

Chapter 9

Felicity

I had only had one day of geography class so far and I hated it so much. But not anywhere near my hatred for precalculus, especially with Mr. Wagner for a teacher. I wasn't disappointed for arriving late for geography, but Toma was. Her mouth shut mid-sentence during the lesson and she glared at me. "Do you know how late you are?" she squealed in her old-woman voice.

I looked at the clock hung on the wall at the other side of the room. It was a quarter to nine. "Fifteen minutes isn't so bad, is it?"

Toma looked bewildered. "Have a seat and don't bring that attitude to class."

Damn, she was pissy. *What? What did I say?* I took a seat silently, not sure what she meant by "don't bring that attitude to class." I didn't even have one. At least, I didn't think I did.

"So," Toma started. I thought she was going back to teaching her lesson but instead: "Who can tell Felicity what we're learning about in Unit One?"

Was she kidding?

"The structure of the earth," announced the girl from beside me.

Toma put her hands behind her back and straightened her shoulders like a military general. "And, Catrine, what are we studying first?"

Her trooper answered, "Coastal zones."

General Toma turned to me then. "Did you get that?"

I nodded. What the hell?

She said, "Good," and then continued her lesson. "A coastal zone is where land and water meet. They're always changing due to the dynamic interaction between oceans and land."

Toma placed a textbook under the overhead and it showed up on the board. She showed a picture of a beach and the diagram explained where the wave base, circular loops, elliptic loops, the zone of slight erosion and strong erosion, and turbulent water were, and where a wave begins to break.

I opened my binder and jotted down everything the diagram had to offer. The definitions I had to search up on my phone.

"Can anyone guess what the wave base is?" Toma asked.

"The maximum depth at which a water wave's passage causes significant water motion!" I called out, reading from my notes.

"Right." She seemed almost surprised I "knew the exact definition" of something she never spoke of. She expected a guess. Not a straight answer. I didn't know what a wave base was, along with very likely everyone in the class.

"What's erosion?"

I waited for someone else to give the exact answer until I realized the teacher's eyes were set on me. "Are you asking *me?*"

"It's the process of—"

"I wasn't asking you, Kennedy," Toma snapped.

Kennedy shut right up.

"What's erosion?"

I didn't need my notes for this; we had all learned this in the previous year or two. "The process of eroding or being eroded by a natural force."

"But what does 'eroding' mean?"

"Gradually wear away."

"Good."

Now she was asking two new people to define a turbulent and a breaking wave. Kennedy knew what a wave base was, but Darwin had no clue what a breaking wave was.

I changed into my PE strip and went out the side doors at the other end of the hallway and went behind the school to the baseball diamond on the massive field, where we were meant to meet for the next two weeks. Another student joined me in the run to the rest of the class.

"You're on the field," Moretti said to the girl, and to me, "Felicity, you're batting."

I placed myself at the back of the line.

"No, you're batting, as in right now."

"Oh."

She arranged us in our batting order, the same order we would remain in for the entire unit.

I picked up the bat off the loam and readied myself for the pitcher to pitch. Will, who had a black eye like I expected he would, chomped down on his bottom lip with a hint of hate flaring in his eyes. He forcefully chucked the ball, and I hoped desperately my reflexes would be fast enough to swing and hit it—

"Felicity!" freaked an echoey voice.

I peered through my barely-opened eyelids at circling, blurring figures. "Yeah!" I muttered, having zero strength to talk properly. "What... happened?" I forced my eyes open fully and everything around me turned clearer; the circle of images slowing to a stop, the amount of people dividing in half, and my vision wasn't as blurry. I lay on my back and gazed up at Moretti, my classmates, and someone who I presumed was the school's nurse; he held my wrist, checking my pulse. "You got smoked in the head," Moretti answered my question.

My hearing was still off. "I can't hear very well." And I sounded more echoey to myself.

"It will take a while," the nurse told me, "but that's not the biggest concern. Are you dizzy?"

"I was a moment ago."

"How many fingers do you see?" With his free hand, he showed me three.

"Three."

The number of fingers changed. "One."

"Four."

"Five."

"Two."

"Can you see straight?" he asked next.

"Yes."

"Headache?"

"My head just started pounding now."

"Felicity," sang a familiar voice.

I sat upright, causing my head to pound harder and I could hear it. "Did you hear that?"

"Hear what?" Moretti asked, concerned.

"Felicity." It was just plain wispy that time. "That."

Everyone looked as confused and alarmed as me.

"You're just hearing things," the nurse shared his thoughts. "The ball knocked you out for ten minutes. We'll get an ambulance."

"No, I'm okay."

"We should get her an ambulance," Moretti agreed.

I was immediately getting pissed. "I've been through this sort of thing before. I *know* I'm fine." And to prove it, I got to my feet. I felt slightly wobbly, but forced my body still to hide it.

Everyone just stared, worried as hell. "Are you sure you're okay?" the nurse asked.

I nodded. "What exactly happened?" I wanted to change the subject.

"Will accidently hit you in the head," Moretti explained with a touch of sadness in her voice. "He felt bad and took off somewhere."

Accidently. I wasn't going to tell her that it was no accident. I was going to handle him like the vigilante I was.

Chapter 10

Janessa

Mr. Wagner handed our quizzes back and my mark wasn't a surprise at all. I didn't study, but how could I have if he just gave it out without a warning? And what made it worse was that it was for marks.

Putting my quiz aside, I put my attention back on the first lesson of the first unit: functions and relations.

Two minutes later, the bell went and I packed up and went to the cafeteria. I sat at a hidden table to avoid the—what Felicity called them—A-S-S Squad. It was what we'd been doing since Tuesday, the day after the fallout. From my mini blue backpack, I took out a mini container containing a red velvet cupcake. I opened it and licked the fluffy icing.

Felicity joined me. "Hi," she said unfriendly, dryly.

Then came Allison. "Hey."

Mouth full of cupcake, I could only wave.

We were quiet for a moment, just eating away peacefully, until Allison broke the silence. "There's something I have to tell you guys." She turned freaked, and Felicity and I were waiting for the presumed-to-be-disturbing conversation. "Last night, I had a *very* weird dream." She crossed her arms on the table and leaned in to prevent eavesdroppers from listening in. "I was walking on a street in an area I've never been before. I was completely alone, and then I turned a corner and wandered down a street that seemed to go on forever. There was… nothing around… I don't know." She scrunched up her face and shook her head violently.

I turned to Felicity, her face replicating mine of suspicion. What was so bad about a dream?

Allison continued with, "And then I looked back and forward again… and there was this really creepy house that popped up out of nowhere, and it instantly turned to night, and then there was this very high-pitched scream and it woke me up. And I saw… a shadow in the middle of the room. It was giggling and it sounded… I don't know. And I screamed and my mom came in and when I turned to her and then back at the shadow, it wasn't there. I don't know what the hell was happening."

So, the dream was weird, but the reality of the shadow was alarming. I looked to Felicity again and her lips parted. "What did it sound like?" she asked, leaning in, as if she was trying to solve a mystery by forcing Allison to come up with some sort of description of the sound the shadow girl made.

Allison hung her head, probably feeling sick from the ghostly experience. "Like… wispy, if that's the right word."

Felicity's green eyes widened in shock. "I know *exactly* what you're talking about."

All this was making me feel nauseous, though I had no clue what was happening. Allison looked sick. I kept calm to make myself and my friends feel at ease, though maybe there was nothing to feel at ease over.

"The first time I heard it was Monday," Felicity's story began. "I was sitting in my room when I heard a wispy voice saying my name. It said it twice and then it went away. But I didn't see it. Or *her*. And I didn't hear it until PE. I asked everyone if they heard something, but they didn't. Only I did. But they thought I was just hearing things because I was hit in the head—"

"Hit in the head?" I interrupted.

"Yeah. Will threw the baseball directly at my head and knocked me out." My jaw dropped.

"What? I've been through worse and survived. Relax."

Worse? I closed my mouth and let half my brain think about the possibilities of her darkness and the other half hear her finish with, "Anyway, I know I heard it."

The girls turned to me, wanting to hear about my involvement in all this. "Well, I haven't heard anything, but back on Tuesday, I had random internal bleeding, and I felt as if someone reached into my chest and squeezed my heart. If any of that has anything to do with this." I gestured at them and their ghost stories. And Allison looked like she was going to puke and Felicity looked more serious than usual about our unexplainable situations.

"My maids called 911, and by the time the paramedics came, the bleeding stopped."

They glared at each other. "This is too fucking weird," said Felicity, her tone darker than normal.

"What the hell is happening?" I asked shakily. I was calmer before, and now I was losing my mind to the point of feeling faint.

"Do you believe in ghosts?" Allison asked us, her voice and face implying she meant what she asked.

Felicity smirked, clearly thinking it stupid. I agreed with her one hundred percent.

"Well, I do."

My eyes narrowed on my sudden-ghost-believing friend. "You do?"

She chuckled nervously. "How else do we explain this?"

Felicity and I fell quiet, knowing we couldn't argue with her. But I never considered ghosts real. I still didn't.

"I think it's out to get us for some reason." She shuddered as she concluded with, "I think we're in trouble."

"For what reason?" Felicity asked, exasperated.

"*Some* reason."

"Do either of you hear anything now?" I asked.

They eyed each other and listened hard. Felicity asked her, "Do you see anything?"

Allison's eyes roamed the bit of the cafeteria visible to us like a spy. "No."

"So," Felicity began the investigation, "this all began on Monday with me, then on Tuesday with you—" she looked at me— "then last night with you"—she looked to Allison. "Nothing happened to me on Tuesday or yesterday."

"Nothing happened with me on Monday or yesterday," I added.

"Nothing happened with me on Monday or…"

We all stared at each other. "It's following us individually," Allison declared. "We have to figure out what it wants."

"We don't *know* if it really is a ghost," I said.

"There's no other explanation," Felicity remarked. Her face aimed downward, but then her eyes flicked up at me. "Allison's right. We have to figure out what it wants."

I shook my head at the—what I wanted to call it—nonsense. "You're not *actually* believing this." I glared hard at her.

"Yes, Janessa, I am."

I rolled my eyes. "Let's just talk about something else. What did you do in biology yesterday?"

Allison stared at me as if I was an idiot. "You can't just brush this off. But we started—oh, you need to get together to work on it."

"On what?"

"The project."

They explained the criteria to me, and Felicity and I agreed that we were going to meet up after school on Friday so we could put the presentation together. I was excited to *kind of* hang out with Felicity for the first time. And Alex would be overjoyed to meet her.

Chapter 11

Allison

There really was some kind of spirit stalking us. It wasn't a question. It was a statement. But how could I have been the only one who could see it? Or maybe not. Was someone else seeing it, too? Was someone else involved? I didn't know what to think of this. I was too freaked out to know anything. And all these paranormal things my friends and I were experiencing were incomprehensible: the voice only Felicity and I could hear, Janessa having internal bleeding, and me seeing the ghost girl.

"So, you think I'm right?" I asked in almost a whisper.

"About what?" Felicity's volume matched mine.

"That there's a ghost stalking us?"

She lifted her eyes from the Spanish textbook and stared forward. "I do."

"What are we going to do?"

She turned her head forty-five degrees toward me and looked me directly in the eyes.

"Do we call the police?"

"And what? Tell them we're being haunted?"

I looked down. She was right; they wouldn't believe us.

"We have to find out who it is—well, *was*—and find out what it's after. Exactly like what you said."

"How exactly are we going to do that?"

"How do you find a ghost?"

I considered the question thoughtfully. "I don't think we find it. I think it finds us."

Felicity shook her head at herself. "Obviously."

I thought for a second. "Maybe we can communicate with it. Ask what it wants."

Felicity nodded. "I just feel we should be careful communicating with it. If we say the wrong thing, it might get pissed and kill us."

I scoffed. "I'm more worried about Janessa than us. She could actually *die.*"

Her eyes went back to the textbook, but the conversation wasn't over yet. "I'm scared." My voice was rough, like my vocal cords were wearing out.

Her head turned to me fully. "Me, too, but I believe we'll get to the bottom of this."

My heart jumped. *Felicity was scared?* That was kind of surprising. She didn't look it. "We have to," I declared, "or we might die."

"We won't die."

I lost contact with her eyes, not sure if I should have trusted her on that, but I thought I had to have some faith like her to get through this—whatever this really was—and trust her. I was forcing myself to trust her.

She went back to reading again.

With a weak smile, I said kind of jokingly, "I didn't think you felt fear. You don't show it." Was it a weird observation to speak of? Maybe, but she accepted it.

"This is the first time... in years." She raised her eyebrows and widened her eyes, making the face of regret. Did she regret her words for some particular reason?

"When I was thirteen, I learned how to not be so scared under any circumstances."

I frowned. "Why?"

It took her a long time to answer.

"I've been going through heartbreak for five years. At thirteen, I quickly learned that certain emotions—sadness, fear—can weaken you. To stay strong, I had to push those feelings aside. It seemed like the only way I was going to live."

"But... we all get those feelings." Nothing was making sense anymore: the ghost, or Felicity herself.

"Not me," she said sharply. "Not anymore."

"Until today."

She stared at me and I couldn't figure out what she was meaning to say with her stare. But whatever. "What happened?"

"I'm reading" was her excuse.

"City," I decided to call her all of a sudden. It was her nickname anyway, and I wanted to make her feel that she really was my friend. "Janessa and I are your closest friends. You can tell us anything."

"I will eventually, but not now."

Honestly, my heart sank. I desperately wanted to know what had been troubling her for so long, what troubled her so much that she forced herself to become impenetrable. I thought the decent thing to do would be to explain her issue in the same amount of detail I had given about my past with Joy and my father. But I didn't want to be the sort of person who pried into someone's seemingly tragic life, so I had to respect Felicity for it. "Okay."

Out of respect of me respecting her, she gave a slow nod.

Chapter 12

Felicity

It was midnight when I was still studying for an upcoming Spanish quiz. I was too creeped out to sleep. The night was a hell of a lot scarier knowing a demon from Hell was after me. I had my desk lamp on, plus the ceiling light, the brightness not making much difference on my nerves. Occasionally I would look around the room to be sure all objects were in their rightful places. If they were in different spots, that would be a sign the ghost was right there with me. It could have been standing next to me. Or maybe it was roaming the rooms of my house. But I didn't want to know.

I was scared to be alone. Dad was still at the party for his friend's daughter's first birthday. I had no clue when he would come home and I didn't care. I would stay up all hours of the night. I wasn't going to sleep until he returned.

"Felicity."

I jumped from my chair and backed into the wall. "WHAT THE FUCK DO YOU WANT?!" I bellowed with fear and rage. My heart created a storm so horrific that my blood circulation was corrupting my sight and focus, and my heart dared me to dart out the door and get out of the house. But where would I have gone?

"Fel-i-ci-ty," the ghost sang.

I accepted the dare and charged for the door. But what must have been invisible hands clung onto my shoulders and pulled down. I fell onto my bottom and the pull pulled me onto my back. The ghost could touch me. I fought to get to my feet and flee, but the dead stalker's hands kept me down. She laughed hysterically as I tried to claw at her hands and grab them to free myself, but I was only clawing and grasping my shoulders. I kicked my legs up and over my head to kick her off me, and if I did kick her, my feet went right through her. Me trying to fight off the dead freak was like attacking the air.

Remembering I had to be tough at all times, I pushed to get off my back, the weight of what appeared to be nothing weighing me down. The ghost and I had a battle of who was stronger, me winning… I won.

As I thundered down the stairs, the ghost called, "I'll count to ten. One…" The cushioned chair blocked the door, trapping me in. The ghost put it there to prevent me from escaping, and there was no time for me to push it out of the way before she caught up. I had to hide. We were playing hide and seek, after all.

Thinking fast, I ran behind the staircase to the kitchen and hid around the corner. I looked to the knife holder. I pulled a large knife from it, making a quiet *shing*. Though it was useless, I felt some kind of comfort with a weapon in hand.

"Where are you, Felicity?" the ghost sang.

I suddenly had a plan. I jumped out of my hiding place. "Here!"

I waited before acting.

"Oh, there you are," she squealed wispily.

I brought the knife up to my throat and pressed it against my skin, hard, but still able to breathe. If she tried to take it from the angle that I held it in, she would slit my throat. This was how I would have her spill all her answers to me; by faking suicide. She wanted me and my friends for something. She couldn't use me if I was dead.

"No, wait!" There was a shake in her voice

"WHO THE FUCK ARE YOU?! TELL ME OR I'LL KILL MYSELF!"

"I… can't tell you quite yet."

"Really?" I taunted. I pressed the knife only a little harder against my throat, still allowing lots of air to pass through my windpipe, threatening her.

"Don't kill yourself!"

"Start talking," I wheezed.

"I need you!"

"Still waiting."

"You have to wait longer."

I dragged the knife about two inches.

"Stop! I'm a girl who needs help! Well, I was twelve when I died. That's all I can tell you right now." The next part was calmer: *"Before I can give more of an explanation, you and the others have to prove yourselves."*

"Prove ourselves?"

There was a moment of silence.

"I have a task for you and your friends. But first, I need to see how strong your friendship is. And if I like what I see, you'll play my game. And then I'll assign you the task."

"You can't use me if I'm dead ."

"I'll make you a deal; don't kill yourself and show me how strong your bond with Janessa and Allison is, and all this will be over shortly. Die, and they die, too."

My eyes widened, and my feet became numb and I slumped against the counter for support. I was pretty sure my heart gave its last beat and my blood circulation stopped. I lost the tiny bit of strength it took to hold a knife and dropped it. It *clanged* hitting the floor.

The dead girl continued. *"Selflessness is a very powerful thing. Go through some torture for them to live and they'll do the same for you. If one dies, you all die. Do you accept my deal?"*

I nodded weakly. "Yeah, but this all so stupid. You're harassing us because you want to see how strong our bond is."

"Maybe this is dumb to you, but believe me when I tell you I have very good reason."

"What's the reason?"

"You'll find out."

"What's the game we have to play?"

"You'll find that out, too."

"What about the task?"

"You'll find that out, too."

I felt like passing out.

"I'm off now."

I regained a slight amount of consciousness. "You're off now? Where are you going?"

I heard movement and looked to the door. The cushioned chair slid back to its spot "by itself."

I waited a terrifying moment before collapsing onto the floor beside the knife, a couple of drops of blood beneath the blade. But I didn't care about my throat. It probably wasn't going to scar. And I did something I haven't done in years: weep. And felt something I hadn't felt in years: fear. My friends and I were in danger. No one could help us. We only had each other. But I thought as long as we cooperated with the ghost, we would live. I was too scared to, though. But I was in possession of Janessa's and Allison's lives. I felt like it was going to be pure hell to play with the ghost and possibly death. I feared for mine and my friends' lives.

Chapter 13

Allison

"How were your classes this morning?" I asked Janessa, simply making conversation at the start of lunch.

"Pretty good. I'm starting to dislike my math teacher, though."

"You've only had three classes with Mr. Wagner and you're already disliking him?"

"Pretty much, but I'm not ready to fully dislike him. I usually give some time before figuring out who I like and don't like."

I nodded in understanding.

"But Felicity might not like hers either."

"Why do you say that?" I asked.

She pushed a chunk of hair back over her shoulder. "She just... seems that way."

I totally agreed. "She doesn't seem to like anyone."

I considered something for a moment. "That must have been a result of the tragedy."

Janessa leaned forward, the chunk of hair falling over her shoulder again, eyes narrowing. "What tragedy?"

"She wouldn't tell me. What she did tell me, though, was that she's going through heartbreak and that at thirteen, she learned how to not feel emotional."

"So… no sadness, fear…?"

I nodded, probably feeling the same way as Janessa.

She looked elsewhere. "That's not right."

"It's good to learn to toughen up after a tragic event, but not to the point of being… impenetrable. And not to be rude or anything, but she appears to be hateful."

"So, whatever happened really took a toll on her."

Past Janessa, I could see Felicity storming to our table. She stood at its side. "We need to talk." She sounded scared.

"O-kay," I started. "Have a seat." It was right after those words I noticed a two-inch cut on her throat. *Where did that come from?*

"Not here. Somewhere private, where no one would be."

Janessa and I looked at each other. *Somewhere no one would be?*

"The basement," Felicity declared.

"Our school doesn't have a basement," said Janessa.

"Every school in Ravendale does." Felicity took her phone out of her purse and was doing something on it…

"Okay, this way."

Without question, Janessa and I picked up our bags and followed Felicity out of the cafeteria to the unheard-of basement, all the way to the other side of the school.

We came to a staircase leading to the top floor, but there was no basement.

"I don't get it," said Felicity. "There should be a door here."

Instinct told me to look behind the staircase. Against the wall were cardboard boxes stacked upon each other. I unstacked them, seeing more of the door with each box moved aside. *What the hell?* "Found it." The door was metal with a tiny window near the top, so dusty the window was almost black. *Was this always here?* I'd spent my high school years here and I found out about the basement *now?*

Janessa and I glanced at each other, and based on how she looked at me, she didn't know about this either.

Felicity gently pushed me out of her way and turned the knob and pushed the door open, widening with a groan painful to the ears. The room before us was black. I turned on my phone's flashlight and shined it into the blackness, Janessa and Felicity following suit. "Stairs," Janessa observed and entered through the door. We descended them single file—

The door. I went back to shut it, just hoping nobody would see it if they decided to randomly look behind the stairs. And what if someone had put the boxes back? We wouldn't be able to get out.

Also, knowing there was a ghost after us, this was the last place I wanted to be.

I aimed my flashlight downward and followed the lighted stone steps. I couldn't explain how petrified I was. I could hear my own heart screaming at me to get the F out.

When my shoes touched the stone floor, I saw there was a long hallway ahead, which I didn't want to go down. "Is this private enough for you?" I snapped at Felicity out of absolute horror.

"I'm scared as shit, too, Allision," she snapped back. "Let's try to find some light. Like a switch or—"

"Found it," Janessa informed. The sudden explosion of light made me scream and it rang down the stoned hallway.

"Let's make this quick," Janessa said briskly to Felicity, "before she passes out."

"It came to me last night," Felicity started, voice breaking.

"The ghost?" I asked nervously.

Felicity teared up and nodded. Janessa and I stared. We never expected Felicity to be like this.

"What happened?" Janessa asked desperately.

"She told me she's after us."

Janessa and I took turns asking questions. I went next. "Why is she?"

"She wants to see how strong our friendship is."

"Why?" Janessa asked next.

Felicity shuddered, looked down, shook her head, and black tears from her mascara streamed down her cheeks. "She has something planned for us."

"What does she have planned?" I was drowning in horrid sickness.

"Something that involves life and death. Our lives are in each other's hands."

"I-I-I-I'm not following," I stuttered, stealing Janessa's turn.

Felicity took a seemingly painful breath and laid everything out: "She has a task for us to do for her. I don't know what it is. But first, she wants to see how strong our bond is, and once she does, we have to play some kind of death game, and I guess if we win, she'll assign the task."

Feeling faint, I collapsed with a loud smack on the hard, cold stone. Janessa came to me and sat on her knees and held me. "Allison, we'll get through this," she tried to assure me.

"We're going to die! This is a death trap! The ghost has control of us and no one can help us!"

"So, if we lose the game, we *die*?" Janessa asked Felicity sheepishly.

"Sounds about right."

"OH, MY GOD!" I wailed, monstrous tears pouring.

"Let's not worry about that now," Felicity insisted. "The ghost wants us to reveal a strong bond, and by doing that, we have to stay absolutely strong... and survive for one another. If one dies, we all die."

"I'm sure as hell not surviving this!" I shrieked. I really felt as if I was about to pass out, but I forced myself to stay conscious.

Felicity sat on her knees in front of us. "She's got us—you're right, Allison—but we can make it. We just have to do exactly as she says and we have to stay alive. No matter how fucked up this is, we have to go through it. We don't have a choice. And I'm not sure whether the ghost meant it or not, but she said that if we follow along, it will all be over shortly."

That's definitely not true. I shook my head wildly. "No, no, no..."

"Felicity's right," Janessa said calmly, looking down at me. Her voice didn't match her face. "We have to do this." Janessa released her tears with me and Felicity.

"Who's the ghost?" I asked.

"She's a twelve-year-old. *Was.* That was all she said about herself." Felicity studied the basement. "This is where we'll meet to talk about all this. It's too risky to talk about this where people will eavesdrop and think we're idiots and report us to social services. But we come down here together. Not alone."

Janessa and I nodded.

"Remember, we have each other and we'll help each other survive the torture."

Torture.

"How do you know we'll make it?" Janessa asked.

There was a long pause.

"I have... faith. One other thing: we keep this between ourselves."

Like who would believe us, anyway.

Chapter 14

Janessa

Felicity followed me to one of two of the school's parking lots. I hopped into the driver's seat of my car and she sat in the passenger's seat. Putting the keys in the ignition, I said, "We just have to wait for my brother."

"No problem."

A few minutes passed in silence before Alex stood at Felicity's window, not expecting to see someone in his spot, and stared lovingly at the girl who stole it. I guessed she felt uncomfortable because after a few seconds, her head slowly turned away to me, a look of disturbance perfectly clear. I looked past her and mouthed "get in." He hopped into Luke's spot and put his navy-blue backpack in Lee's. "You never said Felicity was coming over," he said with excitement.

"We have a project to do," I said, pulling out of the stall and straight down the two-lane road and then into traffic.

"How does he know me?" Felicity asked.

Alex answered, "I saw you fight Cody and Will back on Monday. Pretty impressive. No one has ever stood up to them before."

"How hard is it, exactly?"

"Very. Everyone knows disobeying them leads to bad shit."

"Yesterday in PE, Will knocked me out with the baseball. I'm sure they're all after me now."

"Really? Such assholes. They're worse than I thought."

"I'll be fine, though."

"He didn't get suspended?"

"He claimed it was an accident."

I bet Alex was really enjoying his and Felicity's first chat. It wasn't a good one, but they were still having it.

"You didn't tell the principal?"

"I can handle shit on my own. Plus, I have something far worse to be concerned about."

Okay. That made sense.

"Can I ask what?"

I came to a red light when my friend and I took a look at each other, the same thing on our minds.

"What?" Alex asked desperately. He wanted the talk to go on until forever.

Neither of us answered, and he respected the private scenario. So, he continued with, "Kick his ass when you get the chance."

The light turned green and I stole a quick glance at Felicity. She stared dumbly out the windshield, not wanting the dark subject to go further.

"How was your first week?" I thought it a good thing the topic changed to something uplifting.

"It was good. I don't like geography, though."

"I hate math and science," Alex said.

"I think everyone hates math, and school in general."

"I don't know one person who actually likes school."

I didn't belong in the conversation, but... "Allison does."

"Strange," he judged.

We pulled in through the gates and I slowly drove around the fountain and parked behind Denise's car. We all got out and Felicity studied my white and creamy yellow mansion, the tall blue-tinted windows on either side of the double doors, and some of the balconies in awe. "Whoa."

I smiled and ascended the soft stone stairs to the door, she and Alex following. And her eyes really lit up once we were inside. She examined the pale brown floor, the large indoor balcony edged with gold wavy-styled railing, the large staircases leading upstairs to two hallways edged with the same railing as the balcony. The massive living room to the left and the massive dining room and the kitchen to the right. And the crystal chandelier hanging over us with the sun shining through the big pentagon window, and its shine reflected onto the marble floor. And past the stairs, the gaming room. "This is amazing." She seemed amazed, but there was no change in tone.

"Thanks," mine and Alex's voices overlapped.

Luke, Lee, and Caleb came up to us from the gaming room to greet Felicity. "Hello," Lee and Luke said. But Caleb looked up at her, timid, which made sense, given how Felicity had a seemingly natural intimidating appearance. He reached blindly for Lee's hand, eyes never leaving her. He found Lee's hand and gave it a good squeeze and Lee gently brought him to his side and hugged an arm around him, but was smiling, knowing Caleb didn't need any protection. But Caleb dipped his chin and dug his face into Lee's leg, his slightly long blond hair concealing his frightened brown eyes.

"Hi, I'm Felicity," Felicity said to the three boys, more so to the six-year-old.

"I'm Lee, and this is Caleb," Lee introduced the two of them.

"And I'm Luke."

Denise and Malia came out from the kitchen and saw Felicity. I didn't know where Kira was. They came over. "Hi," Denise started, sticking her hand out, "I'm Denise."

"Felicity." Felicity shook her hand, not smiling.

"And I'm Malia." They shook hands, too.

By their black dresses and white aprons, it was clear to Felicity that they were maids.

"It was nice meeting you, Felicity," Alex said before walking up the stairs on the right.

"Likewise."

Alex disappeared behind the wall of the hallway.

After all the "nice to meet yous"—not from Caleb—I led her up the stairs on the left to my room at the end of the hall. She stared in awe for the third time, loving my massive bedroom; the pink walls so pale they almost looked white, my queen-sized bed, glass double doors leading out to the circular balcony, my vanity, walk-in closet, desk, bookshelf, posters and framed pictures, a fluffy bean bag chair, and a couch. "Holy sh..." She got lost in speech.

I laughed.

"Explain."

"Mom's a singer and Dad's an actor."

"Wow."

I smiled, but some sadness lay behind it. "It's kind of sad, though."

"How?"

"My brothers and I don't get to see them as much as we'd like to."

Felicity nodded. "Do you want to get to work?"

"Yeah." I took my laptop out of my desk drawer and sat next to Felicity on the couch. "Send me Allison's map."

I received it and put it on a PowerPoint slide. As we listed the ways to be safe in the science classroom, I considered asking her about her summer. Yeah, it was kind of late to be discussing that *now*, but she wouldn't tell me or Allison what she'd been up to. "So, how did you spend your summer?"

"Behind bars."

What the hell? What was that? I glared darkly at her, almost feeling like her.

A few seconds passed before she glared back at me and stood. Mentally preparing herself to spill the events of her past life, her secret, she walked slowly to my shelf and picked up a photo of me and Allison from some years back. "I used to be innocent… Happy. But when my mom died, my life spiraled out of control. A year after her death, I got myself into bad shit and my personality totally changed. I taught myself how to not be intimidated by certain things, and people, so I could remain strong, and I believed dark makeup helped create a dark impression. That all backfired. I made new horrible friends—since I lost the old ones—and we got in trouble with the law: doing graffiti, robbing from local stores, and abusing drugs, but drug abuse didn't last too long." She looked to me then. "One night when I was high, I mugged someone and was put in jail for two months."

I couldn't believe what I was hearing. "Oh, my god."

"They also taught me how to fight enough for me to defend myself against other druggies. That happened once. And when I was released from prison a few days before school started, my dad and I moved here from Thumber, in hopes I can start over and have a better life." Felicity put the photo down, but kept looking. "Nowadays, I just want to be left the hell alone, so I'm keeping this… personality of mine. And I'm used to it. It's natural now."

"Do you still wear makeup because…?"

"No. I wear it just because it's what I'm used to. But I have to wear dark lipstick and a lip ring to hide a scar, from another night of getting high."

"And why aren't you… friendly?"

"Again, it's what I'm used to. Also, speaking the way I do. Looking at people the way I do—that's just me."

I was probably digging too deep into this, but… "Do you have self-hatred?"

"No." Felicity took a few steps closer to me to stand in front of a family photo hanging on the wall. "But I don't like myself either."

"Do you hate people?"

"Only those who piss me off. The Ass Squad would be a good example."

This was the most emotional chat I ever had with someone. Honestly, I felt like breaking down, but seeing this severely troubled girl shedding no tears stopped me from letting a few drops that had built up fall.

"How did she die?"

"Car accident."

Did she mind I was asking all these personal and depressing questions? Maybe it was time to stop. I shook my head and dropped my face to my laptop. "I'm so sorry." I sounded so quiet she may not have heard.

"Thanks."

I kept my face down, but strained my eyes to see her coming back to my side. "You know? Allison doesn't have—"

"A father. She told me."

Maybe I could ask… "Does she know?"

"No. I wasn't ready to talk about it."

That didn't make a lot of sense. Allison told Felicity about her past… but Felicity didn't tell her about her own? Maybe Allison hadn't told her everything. I wasn't going to tell Allison that Felicity had a real dark side to her. She wouldn't like how her two friends, best friends, were talking about her behind her back. It wouldn't be entirely wrong, but she wouldn't like it.

Another thought: "Maybe you should tell her." I spoke very quietly for this part: "That will help prove how strong our bond is to the ghost. Maybe she feels we're too secretive and that we should know each other's dark secrets."

"What's yours?"

I wasn't prepared for that. "I don't have one."

"Whatever. We're not talking about that *now*. We have a project to do."

Seeing I wasn't doing any work on my laptop, she sat back down beside me and lifted it from my lap and put it on her own. She just wanted to get on with it. Maybe trying to shove the devasting thoughts aside. "But you're right. I should tell Allison."

She typed away and I thought about how sorrowful her life was. I felt terrible. But the best thing I could do, and Allison, too, was just be her two best friends.

Chapter 15

Allison

I relived the moment of walking down the infinite road. I should have been tired and sore as hell from the second long walk, but I felt fine. Again, I stood before the ghostly-looking house. And again, day turned to night with a snap of fingers. Why? How? But the difference this time was that I was getting farther into this... whatever this was.

I took several steps to the porch with caution like a cat creeping up on a mouse. I glared at the door with cat eyes. My heart should have been beating abnormally, but its rate was normal. I put one shoe on the first step and waited.

With all the weight of my right foot on the step as I stepped off the ground with my left and put it on the next step up, both steps croaked like highly distressed frogs—

The high-pitched scream came.

I woke with a startle. I was farther into that strange dream. Weird.

Sensing someone—not Joy—in the room, watching, waterfalls of fear tears flowed down my temples. I stared up at the top bunk to avoid seeing the demon's shadow.

"Don't even try to avoid me."

"Go away," I pleaded quietly so my sister wouldn't hear.

"When the time comes, I'll be gone forever... well... depending on whether you're going to Heaven or Hell."

"Felicity told me that you want some task completed." A storm of distress occurred and breathing was a challenge. "What's the task?"

"You'll know soon enough."

Why did I think she would answer me when she didn't answer Felicity?

"Come with me."

Rejecting her command would have been fatal, so I went along with it. I sat up and wiped away the tears with the sleeve of my nightgown. Through the dark I could see her shadow disappear through the door. I got up and opened the door to let myself through, nauseous as hell. I trailed far behind to the living room. Ghost Girl sat calmly onto Joy's pink plush beanbag chair, so I had the impression she wasn't going to torture me. It flattened a tad bit due to her weight. How? She was a ghost. She sat cross-legged and pulled the skirt of her white dress—appearing a little grey in the dark—down to her shins. *"I love these."* She referred to the beanbag chair. *"Well, loved. I used to have one."*

Though I was losing a sense of reality, I felt some sympathy for her. Her life had come to an end at such a young age. *Twelve.* She died a child.

I took a seat on the red velvet sofa and looked at the dead girl the exact way I felt.

She continued with, *"My dad gave it to me before he died, and two days later, my sister tore it apart."*

My fear was transforming more into sympathy. "That's horrible," I said quietly.

Ghost Girl nodded emotionally and dipped her chin, her long, tangled black hair falling over her shoulders.

"What happened to him, if it's alright I ask?"

Her chin rose and there was a bit of a frown visible.

"Never mind. It's none of my business." I waved my hands to brush the question off.

"Heart attack."

"I'm so sorry."

"Thank you. I actually got to see him for a moment... you know... after my death." She was very calm.

"What happened to you?"

"I don't want to talk about it quite yet."

Felicity totally would have related to that. I couldn't imagine how rough that visit must have been. But I couldn't be an idiot. She returned from Hell. But still, I felt the sadness hard in this conversation with the dead girl.

"I should be with him right now," she went on, *"but he sent me back because he needs something of me."*

"And that's what you need us for—me, Janessa, and Felicity."

"Correct. And once the job is done, I'll return to him. Forever."

I didn't know what to say to that, so I just came up with, "Whatever you need us to do, we'll do it."

"Oh, I know you will." This was turning dark, and so was her wispy voice. *"We might be having a friendly-but-depressing conversation, but yours and your friends' lives are still on the line."*

Sympathy was slowly transforming back into terror. I took a lung-aching breath. "How do you want us to prove how strong our friendship is?"

"Find out everything about each other. No secrets. Watch each other's backs closely. And push through pain and fear to save one another from death."

Felicity had said something about this. "Are you going to hurt us?"

"You bet. That's what all this is about. But also, if you can protect each other from Maisie, Cody, and those people, that will be a major help in proving your bond. You know how dangerous they are. Especially Maisie."

Yeah, I knew damn well what they were capable of. "Are you going to make them torture us?"

"I could, but I want everyone in their own state of minds for this."

I didn't quite understand, but I didn't ask for clarification.

Ghost Girl might have had information about the hellions. "What's the deal with Maisie, Cody, Elaine…?"

"Maisie is more than just dangerous. She's a complete psychopath."

My eyes widened. That was what Felicity said.

"Cody has a learning disability, and since he's Maisie's boyfriend, he looks up to her for guidance."

"Damn," I breathed.

"Elaine has a rough life. Her mom drinks a lot and it's hard on her and her dad. Both Will and Isla were bullied bad in elementary school. And Daniella's an addict."

I realized I needed my mouth to deliver more oxygen to my lungs. I never really considered my life bad. Felicity's life was because of how she changed negatively after her mother died, but she was trying to fix that. The difference was that Felicity and I were trying to make the best of our lives. The others were letting their negativity get the best of them. They couldn't, or maybe didn't want to, control it.

"How do you know all this?"

Ghost Girl shook her head, meaning she wasn't going to tell.

"Well, do you at least know how Maisie's been doing after the passing of her sister?"

"A lot better."

"What?"

"Like I said, she's a psychopath. She's insane."

My head rolled onto the back of the sofa in total dread. "I don't believe it."

"What don't you believe?"

"How… screwed up they are."

"Bullies don't bully just because they feel like it. They have issues of their own and that's how they deal with them, and when you see the severity of the abuse they cause to others, you understand how severe their own issues are."

I lifted my head.

"They have a problem with you and Janessa more so now because Felicity stood up to them. She's their main target, but they'll still come after you."

I thought back to Felicity sharing the news that Will threw a baseball at her head and knocked her out. Was Ghost Girl mad that neither me or Janessa were there to help? Did she even know?

"This conversation's over." She stood up suddenly and the beanbag chair bounced back up. She headed for the door.

I stood up, too. "Where are you going?"

"None of your business." She walked through the door. Literally.

"Al-son?"

Joy was suddenly there, coming to my side, and my heart leapt. Did she hear anything? Anything at all? "Wh-what's go-ing on?"

"Nothing."

She wasn't buying it.

"Come on. Back to bed."

Chapter 16

Janessa

After push-ups, sit-ups, jogging back and forth in the hallway, and skipping rope, I put on my competition dress. It was purple with long sleeves. There were silver gems circling the hips like a belt. The skirt was satin with another skirt of lace overtop. White fur lined the neck and the wrists. I made it in sewing class at school.

Melinda tugged my hair into a bun and I felt as if she was ripping my hair out her grip was so strong. She added sparkling hairspray to make it stay in place. Then she did my makeup; light pink eyeshadow, rosy pink blush, mascara, and blood red lipstick.

"The group is on in a minute!" she announced to me, Carly, Maggie, and Dessa. The other skaters had to attend the following two competitions due to so many skaters signing up for this one.

I put on my club jacket and followed Melinda and the skaters out to the ice when it was time. The announcer was announcing our names, and once we heard our own, we stepped onto the ice and warmed up with the competition warm up.

We got to do a run-through of our solos before we had to exit the ice. Except for Maggie, the first in our group to go. She removed her club jacket and handed it to Melinda, revealing a blue one-sleeved dress, the skirt having a slit to the hip. It looked beautiful with her French braid bun and slightly dark makeup.

"Please welcome Maggie Blake from Ravendale Skating Club!" the announcer said.

Everyone applauded as Maggie took her position center ice.

Maggie moved briskly, her pace matching her piece of music beautifully. I honestly believed her solo was the best compared to mine, Carly's, and Dessa's, but ours were great, too.

After a few minutes, Carly was on.

Then a skater from Felicity's hometown.

Then another skater from Thumber.

Dessa.

Two skaters from an area I didn't know how to pronounce.

Me. I removed my club jacket and gloves and stepped onto the ice.

"Please welcome Janessa Owens from Ravendale Skating Club!"

I skated to center ice and waited for my slow-paced music to come. I felt some sort of pinching from within. Nerves? No. I felt liquid dribbling over my bottom lip and put the tip of my finger to it. I looked with terror at the blood now on my finger. The ghost was accompanying me at a *really* bad time. I knew I had to hold myself together for only a few minutes. And luckily, my lipstick was the colour of blood, so no one would be able to see what was happening to me.

I held my hands above my head like a ballerina. My ballet music played and I gracefully lowered my right arm, watching it descend to my waist. I curved that hand as if I was cupping something in my palm. I mirrored that motion with my left arm, plus my hand. Keeping them still, I twirled on my toe picks, the music blocking out the sound of crunching ice. I raised my arms and spun around, doing cross-overs to pick up speed for the axel when the music lost its ballet tone. When my leg was bent ballerina-like and the world spun upside down, that horrible pinching and squeezing feeling in my heart occurred. I fell out of the spin and lay on the ice, blood flowing heavily from my mouth.

I cried out in pain and terror.

Screams from the fearful audience were slurs.

I tossed and turned as two people carrying a stretcher, accompanied by Melinda, Carly, Maggie, and Dessa, crouched down beside me and lifted me off the bloodying ice and settled me on the stretcher. They carried me off the ice and away from view, and Carly, as traumatized as I was, squeezed my hand, not caring it was caked in my blood.

My family joined us.

One of the two people called 911.

I was overwhelmed by how this horrible incident happened during a skating competition. Couldn't it have happened somewhere more private? Since I was beyond petrified, I couldn't remain conscious, so I let my eyes close and allowed myself to be consumed by the world of blackness and calm.

Chapter 17

Felicity

I was in the middle of lunch with Dad when my notification ringtone sounded. I stood up from my chair and went to my phone, charging on the counter. Is the ghost with you? Allison texted.

I haven't heard her so I don't think so.

Crap, that means she's with Janessa at her competition.

I was flurried, and my hand shook viciously as I replied with, Where's the arena? If the paranormal freak was with her, that would mean Janessa would have her ghostly internal bleeding disorder in front of countless people at her skating competition, and they would call 911 and she'll be taken to…

Before I let Allison respond, I called Janessa, though there was a high probability she wouldn't pick up.

"Felicity, we're at the hospital! Janessa's dying!" Alex was panicking, and his words were scrambled, but not so much that I couldn't hear them.

"She's *dying*?" I had to pretend that I thought it was true, though there was actually nothing really wrong with her.

"Seems like it." His voice was breaking, as if he was about to cry.

"Allison and I are on our way." I hung up and then called Allison. "Janessa's in the hospital."

"Oh, crap. Can you pick me up at the school? I'm close by."

"See you soon." I hung up and turned to Dad, who was as panicked as I was. "We need to go!"

Dad was listening in on everything from my point of view. "Let's go."

We charged to the truck and I hopped in beside him and said, "We have to go to the school to get Allison."

We arrived in less than fifteen minutes, and Allison bolted over when she saw us coming. She sat behind me.

I prayed we wouldn't get pulled over—not quite stopping at stop signs, driving through a red light when it just changed from amber, speeding… practically everything that would happen in a car chase.

We hadn't entered the parking lot yet when Allison and I threw our seatbelts off. I gripped the door handle, ready to swing it open. Dad skidded to a stop outside the entrance—the tires screeched against the cement—and I threw the door open and let it fly. Allison and I left the doors wide open and I called back, "Wait for us!" We sprinted to the front desk. "We're looking for Janessa Owens," Allison said briskly.

The receptionist looked her up on the computer. "Room thirteen. Go right and it will be the last room on the left."

We took off.

"No running!" she called after us.

We ignored her. People stepped aside to let us through and watched us as if we were maniacs. We turned the corner and all the way at the other end of the hall were Janessa's brothers and one maid standing outside the room.

As we neared, Luke, or Lee, and Caleb looked to us. "She's in there!" Luke or Lee called, though it was pretty obvious.

We slowed to a brisk walk to the group of terrified and concerned faces. They moved places, allowing me and Allison to stand in the doorway and examine a bloodied and unconscious Janessa lying on the hospital bed. There was a thin line of blood from the corner of her mouth to her earlobe. Her figure skating dress was caked in blood, and the dress must have been blue or purple because the blood was darker on her dress than on her face. Her tights were decorated in large blood spots. And Janessa herself looked dead; hands folded on her stomach like a corpse resting in a coffin at a funeral.

"The doctors don't want us to go in," the maid—I was pretty sure she was Denise—said. Was she the one with the accent?

74

"They don't know what's wrong with her," Alex added, and now cried.

I do.

"Apparently she's very healthy," one of the twins added on.

Me being the kind of person who didn't follow rules very well, I walked into the room to stand beside my friend, and everyone left me alone. I lay a hand on top of hers. She was so pale in the face, besides her pink eyeshadow and rosy cheeks, but she wasn't dead. Hell Girl said we had to live for each other, and as long as we went along with everything she told us to do, we would make it. I looked back over my shoulder. Janessa's youngest brother was the only person—thing—insight. He stood in the doorway, looking at me with his scared brown eyes. Mainly because he feared for his sister's life. The other reason being he didn't find me very comforting. Caleb just stood motionless. He might have been in too much shock to speak or cry. I turned my attention back to Janessa. In the few seconds I turned away, some peach returned to her face. She was going to wake any moment.

"You can't be in here."

I turned around fully, facing the doctor. "She's alive," he said seriously. "That's all I can tell you. The rest is not your concern."

I gawked, totally not expecting that. As Janessa's friend, I was protective and responsible for her, so everything about her wellbeing was definitely my concern. But this guy didn't know that a demon from Hell put this girl in mine and Allison's care. But he had a code and I needed to respect that.

"Please step outside."

I wanted to reject him, but this wasn't the time for it. I stepped outside the door and the doctor shut it.

Only Allison was present. Janessa's family wasn't anywhere to be seen. She read my face. "They went to talk to the receptionist."

I took a seat on a leather chair across the hall and Allison sat next to me. I looked at my acrylic nails.

Allison sniffled.

I looked up and saw her eyes reddening. "She'll be fine. *We'll* be fine."

Allison shook her head, terrified by this ghost issue of ours. She looked to me and then past me. Her eyes were focused on something beyond me. "What?"

"She's here."

I turned my head the other way. All I saw was a nurse walking out of a room and down the hall away from us. I remembered, then, that Allison was the only one who could see her. "We need to talk," I said. I rose from my seat and Allison copied. Together, we walked half-way down the hall and into the washroom. Allison gestured to the paranormal psychopath to come in. I locked the door. At the sink, I slammed my fists down on the countertop and stared angrily at Allison's reflection, since the ghost couldn't be seen. "Start talking, Hell Girl."

"*Well, for starters,*" her wispy voice began, "*I'm glad you're both here; by coming to Janessa's aid, you're proving yourselves.*"

Feeling sick, I lowered my head to the sink. Allison quietly started weeping.

"*I'm beginning to approve of all of you,*" the dead girl went on. "*Do you know the important things about each other?*"

I lifted my chin and looked up with my eyes at Allison through the mirror. "Depends on what you mean by 'important.'"

"*Each other's dark histories.*"

Allison jumped in with a rough voice from crying. "Janessa doesn't have one." Janessa herself told me that.

"*What do you know about Allison's?*"

My chin rose a little higher with my gaze still fixated on Allison, who still looked back at me through the mirror. We were both silent.

In an instant, Allison's hands grabbed her throat. She began wheezing. Her body sank to the floor and she was hunched over her knees.

"*I told you—all of you—that you have to live for each other. Time for you to start talking.*"

Allison's face blued as she gripped her throat tighter.

I had encountered a situation like this before; my old boyfriend had to reveal a secret to protect me. The difference was that I wasn't exactly facing death. "I don't know about her past," I admitted.

"*Nothing at all?*"

I shook my head. I discreetly desperately hoped Hell Girl would be reasonable and stop choking my friend, whose face was so blue that she might have died a moment later.

Hell Girl released her and Allison flopped down on her stomach, coughing and breathing heavily. I watched her, not the least concerned about her anymore.

"*You have to know,*" Hell Girl ordered.

Allison raised her head to look at what I couldn't see. "*Do you know of her past?*"

"A little," she coughed out.

The ghost sighed. *"We need to arrange a therapy session where you expose your dark lives. I'll decide when to have it."*

Then came the horrid silence.

"Is she still here?" I asked Allison, suddenly shaken up.

She got to her feet, breathing and speaking normally. "She's gone."

"Then let's go." I unlocked the door to Caleb right there. "She's awake," he said, pink in the cheeks. The tears had finally come.

My heart leapt and I passed him to see Janessa.

"How are you?" I asked, walking up to her.

She was still lying down, but fully alert. "I'm okay. How long was I out for?" She looked to her maid.

"A couple hours or so," she answered.

"I can't believe this happened in front of so many people." Janessa eyed me and Allison with dread, and we felt the same. A ghost attack in front of so many people who knew nothing of it.

Chapter 18

Felicity

I hated art with all my heart. I was behind by one assignment, which was to draw a fantasy scene, which I was working on for the second week. I didn't know many fantasy figures, so I attempted a unicorn. It didn't look like one at all; more like a dinosaur-cat with a long snout and a stick impaling its forehead.

The reason I chose art of all things was that I needed an elective and I despised all the other options even more. One of the options was cooking and I was overwhelmed.

As I drew my disastrous dinocat, I had visions of Janessa's bloodied body and Allison being choked to near death. All this was crazy scary, but throughout the hell Hell Girl was bringing, we had to keep our cool. Clear thoughts are key to good decision-making, which is a requirement to survival.

I sketched trees behind the "unicorn" when metal-scraping sounds brought my attention to a student who was also in my biology class. The guy was an amazing artist. And quite attractive, not that I cared. He sat on the stool, took one glance at my shitty piece of art, and snickered. I couldn't blame him. "What's that supposed to be?" He didn't ask in a nasty way.

"A unicorn."

He grinned with humour, erased it, and took my pencil from my hand and redrew it for me. He didn't ask if I needed help or not. He knew. "Why did you choose a unicorn when they're hard for you to draw?"

I knew an asshole when I saw one; this guy wasn't one. "I don't know much... fantasy."

"What else do you know?"

"Fairies and flying sheep."

He giggled, but I didn't consider it humorous one bit. His long dark blond curls that went halfway down his neck bounced with each giggle.

I watched my pencil move fast among the paper. It didn't take long for him to draw an amazing rearing unicorn, with a long, flowing mane and tail, a pointy horn, and a sparkle in the eye. "Wow, that's good." I said it as a compliment, but with my dry way of talking, he probably thought I was being sarcastic or something. His face was blank, but I fixed it with, "I mean it." He made a small smile.

I reached over to take my pencil back and went back to drawing more terrible trees.

Him just sitting and watching was slowly pissing me off. "Can I help you?"

"Um... no?"

"So...?"

"Why can't I sit here?"

"I never said you *couldn't*," I said slowly.

"I just want someone to talk to."

"No friends in this class?"

"No more than you."

I stopped drawing and looked at him from the corner of my eye.

"So, how do you like this school?" he changed the topic. And I thought it was strange that this guy I never paid mind to suddenly wanted to get involved in my life.

"I haven't quite decided yet." I looked back down at my drawing. I went back at it.

"Made any friends yet?"

That almost triggered me. "Two. If you noticed me in biology class, you would know."

An awkward silence.

"How do you like your classes?"

That was better. "I hate this class, math, and geography. And partially PE because of Will Peters." I assumed this guy would know who Will Peters was. Smiles claimed that everyone in the school knew the members of the Ass Squad.

"Peters is a total ass."

Yep, he knew.

But the next part wasn't about him: "Why take art if you hate it?"

"I need an elective."

"What level of math are you taking?"

"Precalculus." I discontinued drawing to avoid any rude vibes. I met his brown eyes. "With Wagner."

"I recommend getting the hell out."

I simply looked at him without speaking. I didn't want to leave, no matter what was going to happen with my teacher in the future.

"He's not a very good teacher."

I remained quiet.

This guy was trying to make me quit before it went to the extreme. "He's also not fair. Your test mark takes up the majority of your overall mark and if you get a fairly low mark on your test, he'll blame it on you not studying, even if you did."

I finally spoke. "I'm not worried."

He moved on to geography. "And some students don't like geography only because of how strict Toma is."

"Are you taking it?"

"No, but I have friends who take it."

"What are you taking?" This guy was clearly desperate to talk to me, so I might as well have gone along with it. He was harmless.

"Art, precalculus, English, biology, oceanography—hate it—Chinese, PE—with Janessa—and chemistry—with Allison."

I was clueless on what to say about that.

"I think I'll let you work now. Nice talking to you." He was just about to go back to his usual spot, but stayed put to ask, "What's your name?"

"Felicity."

"Felicity what?"

"Hale."

"I'm Tristan Walker." And then he left me be. I felt at ease then. I wasn't sure if I liked this stranger talking to me as much as he did. Did he like me? Probably.

"I'm still freaked out from yesterday," said Allison weakly as I sat next to her.

"Of course you are."

"Aren't you?"

"Of course."

The second bell rang and Ms. Rivera announced that our quiz was today. I felt ready for it, and knowing about Allison's love for school, she was ready, too.

The quiz was a four-page booklet consisting of vocabulary and reading comprehension. I was about to start when a storm of circling images of the ghostly horrors that I couldn't endure bombarded my brain. I tried like hell to shove them away and focus on the quiz, but they were overpowering me.

Giving up, I shook my head furiously, dropped my pencil, picked up my purse, and exited the classroom.

"Felicity, where—? and Ms. Rivera was cut off by the door slamming, which I didn't intend to do.

I speed-walked to the washroom and locked the door. I became nauseated to the extreme. I threw myself over the toilet and erupted a lemonade-and-doughnut-stomach acid smoothie. I heaved and heaved until the second round. It was a much bigger batch. I breathed heavily, regaining my breath.

Feeling I was finished, I went to the sink and cupped water in my hands and rinsed out the sickening aftertaste.

"How appetizing."

My eyes widened so much that I felt like my eyeballs would fall out. Black tears streamed down my cheeks before I had any attempt on fighting them back.

"I'm not sure if you're as tough as you've been letting on," Hell Girl teased. *"Like, look at you. You're crying."*

If I was capable of grabbing her windpipe and choke her the way she choked Allison, I would have gone for it. "I can't fight what I can't see."

"You also can't touch me."

That, too. I remembered when she fought me. I still won, being stronger than her, but it wasn't easy because of how I couldn't touch her.

Bang, bang, bang, bang, bang. "Felicity, are you in there?"

"Let her in."

I didn't want to invite Allison into the danger, but I had no choice. I unlocked the door and she opened it herself and invited herself in.

"I like this," Hell Girl said happily like a psychopath. *"You're watching over each other. But where's Janessa?"*

"She might still be in the hospital." Allison's voice was raspy and she stared fearfully at the ghost.

"*Oh, well,*" Hell Girl sighed. "*At least we're making some progress.*"

Allison's eyes followed the demon to the door. "She's gone." And before I could react, she threw her arms around me from behind and sobbed into my low ponytail. I wasn't used to… hugs and comforting people, but I crossed my arms and gripped her arms to soothe her.

And I began my silent cry again.

Chapter 19

Janessa

It took lots of convincing to ensure my family and the doctors that I was completely normal and okay—well, physically—before I was allowed to go home. Malia was too anxious to send me to school, so I was resting today and yesterday. Same with Caleb. Since he was beyond sick of fear, he chose to stick with me until Malia thought I was okay to return to school.

Yesterday, I spent time with Caleb, while dreading how I wasn't present in biology class to present mine, Allison's, and Felicity's project, but Malia had said she informed the school's secretary that I was in the hospital, so I'll get the mark with the group, but I still wanted to be there. Caleb and I took Dorothy and Belle into the backyard and made brownies later on.

And today was pouring and windy. We were expecting a thunderstorm late in the evening. We watched two movies back to back, and now we were playing a children's video game. Of course, Caleb loved it, but I was bored.

"Do you feel better, Janessa?" he asked from his personal cushioned chair that fit his size. He referred to my frequent internal bleedings, which to him and everyone else was incomprehensible. Besides Felicity and Allison.

"I'm scared as hell." That was the most honest I could have been. "But I think I'll be fine. Please don't worry about me."

Whatever was to come next with the demon, I didn't want him, or anyone, involved. No matter what. The ghost dilemma was for me and my friends to solve.

"But I *am* worried." He sounded choked up.

I looked at him, and he began weeping all over again. It was as if it was becoming the norm for him. I lay the controller on the sofa and said soothingly, "Come," and stretched my arms out to urge him forward.

Caleb rubbed his wet red eyes with the backs of his hands and dashed into my arms and took a comforting seat on my lap. His tiny arms hugged my neck. "You're not allowed to die," he cried.

You're not allowed to die. That did it. My haunted life was going to be a hell of a challenge to live until we could send the haunter back to Hell. I couldn't battle my feelings for three seconds. Heavy tears poured, and I fought to cry soundlessly and said calmly, normally, "Shh… Shhh." I didn't want the maids to come running and freak out all over again just like him. "I'm not going to die." I wasn't sure if that was true or false.

Caleb had to believe me, like how I had to believe Felicity when she said we were going to make it.

The demon said we had to live for each other, but Felicity and Allison weren't the only ones I had to live for. I had a loving family who needed me, too.

And Felicity had to live for her father.

And Joy and Rita needed Allison.

We had more than each other to live for.

I supposed Alex, Lee, and Luke heard Caleb's cries because they came straight to the gaming room when they usually went upstairs to put their backpacks away before anything. They wore worrisome expressions. And they knew exactly why Little Brother was making a small commotion and they joined in on the heartbreaking hugging. Everyone might have been terrified of a bloody fate waiting for me.

Chapter 20

Allison

I took off running down the apparently endless road.

Then came that creepy abandoned house in which I never reached the front door. Quiet as before, I creeped up the croaking stairs, and this time, I reached the door. I turned the doorknob and slowly opened the door. It groaned louder the wider it opened, and the lights welcomed me. I stood in the doorway and did some examination of the inside of the house; the stairs looked as if they were going to crumble. One of two couches had a massive tear in the back. The closet door on the left hung from its hinges. And the large square mirror was framed with silver engravings.

The mirror and the lights were the only lively things in the house. The house was in poor condition.

Hesitantly, I lifted a foot and placed it gently on the wooden floor. There was always a disturbance whenever it was time to go, but the scream didn't send me away yet. I lifted my other foot and placed it right next to my right—

The scream.

My eyes flared open, and a figure stood in my peripheral vision. I turned my head to it to look directly at the shadow. "Joy?"

"*No.*"

"Ahh—" Ghost Girl slammed her hand down on my mouth, cutting me off. "*Shut... up.*"

The room was dark, but light enough that I knew it was morning. So, in the little lightness, Ghost Girl saw my head nod and she removed her hand.

"Time to get ready for school," she sang wispily. The next part she said normally in her wispy voice: *"You forgot to set your alarm."*

"Joy, wake up. I forgot to set my alarm."

Just like that, Joy easily awoke and climbed down the ladder.

We both dressed quickly. I threw on a plain shirt, jeans, and my white denim jacket. Joy put on a white T-shirt over a black long-sleeved shirt and white leggings.

We rushed to the bathroom to brush our teeth and hair.

"Today we have our therapy session," Ghost Girl said cheerfully, taking a seat on the countertop.

"Therapy is for people who have problems and need someone to talk to," I remarked, since she didn't know what therapy really was.

"What?"

I forgot Joy was there. "Oh, nothing. Just… talking to myself."

"You ne-never t-talk to yourself." She watched me suspiciously. I said nothing.

We had a quick bowl of cereal, got our backpacks, put our shoes on, and went to the elevator.

Ghost Girl leaned back against the elevator wall and looked at Joy, her grey flaky arms crossed. I hoped that was all it was. And it was horrific how calm she was, as if she was planning on what to do with my sister. The ghost's head shifted to where I stood. I gave her a look that said "please don't do anything to her." She stared with her pupil-less eyes—only sclera. With a shrug, she asked, *"What?"* Was she playing innocent or did she really have no intention of hurting Joy?

I became fixated on the shiny black elevator floor and pretended for Joy's sake it was only me and her in there.

On the main floor, the elevator said, *"Ding,"* and the doors slid open. I took Joy's hand in mine and dragged her behind me out the building's doors. I was practically trying to flee from Ghost Girl, but, of course, I couldn't run from her.

"What's your prob-blem?" Joy asked nervously.

I covered up the truth with another truth. "We're going to be late."

Joy's friend Molly was right there with her mother, the car parked by the sidewalk. Mom got called in early and needed someone to take Joy to school.

I gave my sister a hug and told her to have a good day. And I was so relieved to watch the car shrinking with distance. She was safe. For now.

"Come on, Allison. We have to catch the sky train."

The ride was going miserably in a scary way; she sat in front of me and stared me down with her sclera the entire way. I stared back, prepared for her to pull a stunt. But to the other passengers, it was as if I was out of it, just staring stupidly at the "empty" seat before me. The way a couple of people looked at me was a tad bit humiliating. In their minds, I was a stupid girl terrified of a simple fuzzy sky train seat. But they didn't know who—what—was sitting on it. No one saw what I saw. Feeling a little safer with their presence, I felt it was okay for me to look out the window at the downtown city of Ravendale. But as the buildings passed by, so did a flashback of Ghost Girl looking at Joy the way she did. I became uneasy for her life, too, now.

The dead girl stuck with me for the duration of English and sociology. My concentration was split between my two classes and the demon from Hell. Horror seemed like normality now. I forgot what ease felt like.

Then lunch came. The damn ghost freak and I found City and Janessa at a table around the corner in the cafeteria. I said, "We have our therapy session now. We're going to the basement." Ghost Girl knew of the basement because I answered when she asked what the most private area in the school was, and that was where the session was going to take place. But since she followed us all over, she should have had known. I asked about that and she said she wasn't always stalking us.

City and Janessa gave each other sick looks, but obeyed. They gathered their belongings and as a group of four, we made our way to the basement.

We pushed the boxes aside to open the door. We descended the stairs in single file. On the stone floor, I looked past my friends to see the ghost grinning like the devil with her hand on the doorknob. "Brace yourselves," I warned.

Slam.

Janessa released an ear-aching scream in the pitch black of the basement. Again, it echoed down the hall we would never have gone down. And when it quieted, we stood still in the silence and darkness, waiting for Ghost Girl to give instructions.

The light flickered on and we all jumped.

"Sorry for the hold up," said Ghost Girl, *"but I had to hide the door."* She descended the stairs, the skirt of her white dress and her black tangled hair bouncing with each step. *"Please, have a seat."*

City and I sat on the freezing stone floor, before Janessa copied, tucking her knees underneath her.

"Let's begin, with… Allison, my favourite."

Favourite?

"Allison, what was the darkest moment of your life?" Ghost Girl circled us with a slow, calm, dangerous pace, her hands behind her back.

I contemplated an answer, and chose my words thoughtfully. "Um…when I was seven, Joy was born." I added, "With a mental disability my parents and I didn't quite catch on to until she was six. Her teacher brought it to our parents' attention. One thing Joy did was pretend to be asleep to annoy her. And she stuttered. Her behaviour was abnormal. We noticed how Joy was stuttering, but we weren't too concerned, like maybe it was something she would grow out of. We became concerned when her teacher talked about it. Our parents took her for testing and the results showed she's mentally challenged." Getting choked up, I inhaled a large chunk of air to help myself continue. "Dad tried to accept that Joy has a mental disability… but… Joy, our mom, and I had to leave and we temporarily lived with Mom's sister. When Mom had enough money, she bought an apartment." The sobs struck and my words were stuck in my throat. "And… we haven't… seen… him since."

I didn't know why at first, but City reached across the circle. I gave her my hand to squeeze, to comfort. Why?

Janessa's chin was deeply dipped. She was bawling her eyes out. She already knew this story, and didn't need or want to hear it for the second time.

"I loved my father once," I added darkly past the sobbing, "but for a long time, I've despised him." My speech was finished with my remaining efforts to keep myself and my friends from being murdered.

"Doesn't it feel good to talk about traumatic events from the past? It relieves tension."

City glared nastily, blindly at the ghost, hearing her from behind me.

"Your turn, City."

"None of your damn business," City snarled.

Whatever secret she was protecting, hiding it was deadly. Her words of defense were deadly.

"Let's see if this motivates you." The ghost stopped behind Janessa and stared down at her intently. It began with a little blood, dripping off her bottom lip and onto her lap, then the amount grew heavy. Janessa wailed, gurgling bubbles of blood, and flipping onto her side. She clutched her stomach and rib cage.

"Leave her alone!" I screamed. I wept the way Janessa wept. Janessa looked to City for help. "Please," she pleaded.

"Alright, stop!" City commanded instantly.

Ghost Freak's face turned back to normal and she went back to walking the circle. Janessa's blood flow slowed to a *drip, drip, drip*. Her dress that was once pink was now painted crimson.

City began her story. "I used to be innocent, loved by everyone, happy as hell. But my life flipped upside down when my mother was killed in a car accident. Everything about me changed a year after her death to help me cope: my appearance and my personality. Everyone hated what I became. I made bad friends and we committed crimes; robbing local stores, graffiti... and I quit baking and ballet."

This was really hard to take in. It made sense now why City was the way she was; such a dark person. And this explained why she was willing to hold my hand; she knew what it was like to lose a loved one. The only difference was that my father wasn't dead. Though both our lives were tough, we were two different people; I managed my pain. She wrecked her life in order to live on through the dread. However, she was trying to come back around.

"My friends were addicts, but I wasn't *really*. I tried drugs and regretted it. I was high one night and had no conscience and I mugged someone. I was in jail for a while."

I could have sworn my heart gave its last beat. I felt dead. I wasn't prepared for any of that.

But Janessa was different. When she should have had been crying, she was pretty calm. Had she known about this already?

It was as if City's story had no end. "Dad couldn't control me, but he also didn't know what to do. Well... until I called him from the prison and told him I'd been arrested. While imprisoned, he bought a house here in Ravendale and found a job. He decided it was time for a fresh start—go to a new school, make new friends, completely start over. So here I am."

Thank God that was over.

"You're the opposite of who you used to be."

"Shut up."

I didn't mean offence by it.

"Oh, no, City. You have to understand how much this startled her," Ghost Girl babied. She looked to Janessa. *"But she doesn't seem to care as much."*

Since Janessa couldn't hear the ghost, City and I had to play telephone between them. I said to Janessa, "The ghost thinks you don't care."

Janessa was alarmed. "I *do* care, but I've heard this story before."

"Why did you quit ballet and baking?" I asked. Was it rude to ask?

"Mom caught me dancing to music and suggested that I do ballet. It would have shattered me to keep going knowing she wasn't there to see me dance. And I quit baking because it was something we'd always done together."

I was blinded by sympathetic tears so much that I couldn't see City or anything. I was completely blind.

"Did your friends teach you how to fight?" Janessa asked.

I thought it was good that Janessa and I were asking personal questions because it was something the ghost would have had wanted to see.

"Enough for me to protect myself and to not be afraid of assholes."

That was why she wasn't scared of Maisie, Cody, or those people. She knew perfectly well how to handle them.

"Is there anything Janessa wants to share?" Ghost Girl asked me and City.

"Is there anything you want to share?" City asked.

"Truthfully, not really." Janessa made glimpses of the basement, letting Ghost Girl know she was answering to her. "Nothing majorly dark happened to me. However, I wish I saw more of my parents. They're almost always away somewhere and my brothers and I tend to miss them a lot. If that counts."

"Yeah, there's not much darkness in your life," Ghost Girl agreed, though Janessa didn't hear.

This was one of the roughest moments of my life, second to the issue with my dad. Maybe it was wrong of me to say this, but I was almost glad to have had the therapy session. I didn't know how long I would have waited until City told me about her past life, if she even was going to… But why did she tell Janessa and not me? Maybe because she felt it would have been easier to talk to a more easy-going person, to see how that person was going to react.

Chapter 21

Janessa

I was only terrified before. Now I was freaking traumatized. Our lives were in each other's hands, but I lost a severe amount of blood just because the demon demanded that City talks about the darkest moments of her life. Why kill just for that? What could she possibly have wanted the information for? She was dead.

Luckily, I had spare clothes in my locker. City retrieved them for me, given how I was covered in blood and the whole school would see me. Also, I couldn't just throw out the dress. It had to be burned to prevent people randomly finding it and making a report to the police of a supposed murder. I changed and folded the dress and put it in my bag. I washed my face in the bathroom Allison and I found in the hallway in the basement. Since it was an emergency, we had to go into the hallway. There was no soap, but I could at least water my bloodied face.

By the end, my face still had a faint smell of copper.

"Okay, let's go," my voice echoed back to my friends and I followed after the echo. City had Allison's arm wrapped around her shoulders to stop her from collapsing like the last time we were here.

The ghost was no longer with us, Allison had said minutes ago, since I couldn't see or hear her.

We went to biology class, not that we would learn anything. School was becoming more of a challenge for me, and possibly for the others, too. While trying to protect each other from death and encountering the ghost, I felt we had become more fixated on that instead of school. But I was trying to manage as much as possible.

We walked into the classroom and the first thing I noticed, since last week, was Tristan eyeing City. Either she didn't notice him or had no interest, she just sat at the table placed directly next to mine and Allison's without looking at the boy still looking.

Mr. Wilson introduced homeostasis, but since my brain was occupied with terror, all I'd learned was homeostasis is… some kind of internal… condition maintained by… things?

And this wasn't the only class that became hell to focus in; it was all of my other classes.

By the end of biology, Wilson announced, "Read the first two pages," regarding the package he gave out. That was manageable. As long as the ghost taunted someone else.

Allison and I departed from City. My next class was history and Allison's was physics. Our classrooms were in the same hallway.

"Have you been spending time with Roman lately?" I asked, just to make conversation.

"Outside of school? Not really. How can I if a spirit is after me? Us?"

"Well, I mean…" I trailed off.

"But once this is all over, we can try to go back to normal."

"Do you think we'll make it?" I did and didn't believe City. I wasn't sure if she knew the difference between dealing with a live a-hole and a dead one. They were two different things.

Allison grabbed my shoulder to stop me and I spun around. Students hustled around us. "We have to believe her, Janessa," she said calmly.

I tilted my head and she read my face.

"I'm starting to believe her because I don't know what to think anymore. You have to relax and understand that sometimes having faith goes a long way."

"Does City appear to be the faithful type to you?" I asked a little rudely, only because I was scared. City said she had faith, but I didn't believe that.

"Never mind that. Just have some."

I hugged my binder tighter, craving for some sort of comfort.

"This isn't the place to be talking about this," Allison remarked, briefly scanning the busy hallway. She crossed the hallway, saying back, "I'll text you later."

I nodded before entering my classroom. And I guessed I should have been thankful to have Maisie and Cody to worry about rather than the demon. Their eyes were the ones watching now.

And the same scenario happened with history—learned nothing.

And the threat of Maisie and Cody lingered on even after the bell rang. "Hey!" Maisie's super-irritating voice called to me.

I slowed to a stop, as did the rest of the hallway. Everyone watched to see what was to come of this. Through the dead silence was the sound of my heartbeat. I turned around to face Maisie. I was less timid by her ever since City demonstrated how to handle people like her, even though she had some years of experience. Plus, my brothers and I shared the same blood; they got into fights once in a while. I'd found myself in violent situations, too, but it was seldom. How was this going to unfold?

Maisie and I stood face to face. "That friend of your—City, is it—? really pisses me off." Each word she spoke was stupid.

I returned her glare, like what City would do. "Why are you telling me this?"

She chewed her lip and scanned all the students watching. "This isn't the place." Her eyes met mine. "Let's take this outside." She and Cody walked in one direction. I walked in the other.

Cody realized I was going the wrong way and leaped into my path. "We's going the other way," he said with his grammar issues.

Knowing I wouldn't win a fight with him, I followed Maisie out the side double doors. He was close behind like a jailor keeping a close eye on the inmate. We went out to the field, where the rest of their squad was. They saw us coming. They were waiting.

I was immediately surrounded by them. Wolves circling the deer.

"As I was saying," Maisie started from before me, "that girl makes me pissy."

"Whatever your issue is, take it up with her."

I let the words out, making two mistakes: one, we had to protect each other, and two, I just triggered them. Outraged by absolutely nothing, Maisie came at me and I hadn't realized she pushed me down with such force until I was down and looking up. I dropped my bag and binder. Everyone stood over me, their shadows blanketing me from the sun.

"That girl humiliated me in front of the whole school." Her tone was troublesome.

"You needed it."

They weren't expecting the comebacks from me. Maisie's foot hovered over my face. "Stop" saved me.

I threw my head back to see Alex and City stalking upside down toward us through Cody's legs. Alex was a little ahead of her. He threw his backpack down and took his hoodie off, readying himself for a fight. Was he, a fourteen-year-old, going to win against two seventeen-year-olds? Or was he planning on taking Maisie?

No, the two teenage boys. Will and Cody left me at the girls' feet, making two gaps in the circle. Things were about to get bloody.

"Is this your friend?" Will asked Alex.

"Sister."

"Even better."

Alex launched himself at him, knocking him backwards and chucked his fist at Cody's nose.

The boys had their brawl and City and I had ours with the girls. I wacked Maisie's foot aside. I was quickly on my feet. I punched her in the eye and she cried out.

I wasn't as good as them, but I managed to get Maisie and Elaine to stay down by striking them in the face.

City finished her fallout with Isla and Daniella.

Now it was Alex versus Cody and Will. But my brother wasn't doing so well. Will was holding him in a way that allowed Cody to land easy blows to his face. Though Alex tried as hard as he could to break free, Will was still much stronger. Alex's eye was closed and blood rained from his mouth and nose.

City jumped in. She wrapped her arms around Cody's neck, swung him to the side, and stuck her foot out to trip him. He was on his back and she slammed her shoe down on his chest, knocking the wind out of him to keep him down. He was gasping for air, but City ignored him and stalked to Will. He backed up and took Alex with him. Alex choked a little from Will's arm pressing against his windpipe. His other arm hugged one of Alex's. "I'll kill him right fucking here!"

"No, you won't."

I didn't know what City had said or done, but Will pushed Alex into her and she caught him. "Piece of shit," Will hissed. I assumed it was for City.

She took one of Alex's arms and wrapped it around her shoulders to support his walking after such a beating. I helped by taking his other. We basically carried him to my car as people, teachers and students, stopped to look at Alex. One teacher asked what had happened, but we didn't pay any mind to anyone.

City opened the passenger door. Then she helped me settle him into the seat. "I'll go get your stuff." City took off back to the field, back to the danger zone.

I stared at Alex. He didn't look back. He stared forward and slightly groaned at the pain.

City came back safely. She opened the back door and put our stuff inside. "Thanks for the help," I said.

She nodded and looked at Alex. "Take care of yourself."

He lowered his chin weakly in response.

City left us, and Alex and I were going home. I briefly made glances to see if he was holding up. Blood was on the seatbelt, but of course I didn't care. He himself was fully alert. He was in serious pain, and he would be tomorrow and maybe the day after that.

Chapter 22

Felicity

I was doing the dishes while Dad left to do some running around. My knuckles were slightly green from fighting Daniella and Isla. I was going to my locker, and passing Alex in the hallway, he told me he had just seen Janessa going outside with Cody and Maisie. He figured Janessa was in shit and wanted my help, knowing I could get her out of there. So, I put my purse and binder in my locker and followed Alex in the direction they went. I was chuffed he informed me—for mine and my friends' sakes. Hell Girl would have been proud as hell to see me coming to Janessa's rescue.

And the therapy session: what Hell Girl had warned us about. I was beyond pissed, spilling my guts to a lifeless stranger. My past wasn't anyone's business. I only told Janessa about it because it seemed like the right time to talk about it. Plus, I thought my closest friends should have had known about it. I was planning on telling Allison at some point, extending on what I willingly told her before. But I was forced. I didn't want to be when I felt it was necessary to inform her that I was a troubled teen who needed help, before coming to live in Ravendale.

Hell Girl was a psychopath, putting our lives in each other's hands, assuming just to have some demonic fun scaring us with death.

"Well, I'm glad our therapy session went well."

I was taken back to the recent moment. "You're sick. You know that?"

"I have a good reason for—"

"WHAT?! WHAT IS IT YOU WANT?!"

"Can't tell you quite yet."

"Go back to Hell."

"I have a good reason for traumatizing you. You'll understand eventually."

I shook my head in fear and irritation.

"I'm proud, though."

I knew what she was referring to. I shut the water off, the last plate in the dishrack. "I thought you would be." I went to take a seat at the table and she joined me. I leaned back in the chair and watched her chair scooch forward. *"I'm impressed with you and Allison. Janessa—not so much."*

I glowered at a spot I figured her face would be. "What do you expect of her?"

"The same as of you. As of Allison. You need to be guarding each other. Something Janessa sucks at."

I didn't say anything.

Hell Girl continued. *"I'm beginning to wonder if she's selfish."*

I smirked. "She's not selfish."

"Explain how she isn't."

I looked away from her and out the window, to the bubble gum sky. With a sigh, I said truthfully, "I don't have an explanation." I set my eyes to the spot I'd been calling her face. "She's just a kind person, On my first day, she invited me to be in her study group with Allison. I knew nobody. Is that not good enough for you?"

"Not even close."

I rolled my eyes.

"But…"

I stared intently.

"…Where's your phone?"

I rose from my seat and retrieved it from the charger.

"Text her your address."

I obeyed, kind of knowing where this was going, what sick thing was going on in Hell Girl's mind. If the dead even *had* minds.

"Good."

My eyes narrowed on her invisible face.

"Now… we just wait."

"For…?"

She launched herself at me. It didn't even take a second.

Chapter 23

Janessa

"Ow." Alex tensed as I wiped the dried blood off his face with a wet paper towel. He was in too much pain when we got home, so we waited until it eased enough for me to fix him. His white shirt was decorated in red dots, reducing in size as they went down the front, and dirt and grass stains on the back. My fingertips were a little red from him.

I threw the paper towel in his garbage can and took another and dipped it into a bucket of warm water. I wiped up the remaining crimson that blended into his light skin tone. Throwing it out, I said, "You took quite a beating."

"No shit." Alex peered at me with his swollen eye, as much as it could open. By tomorrow, it would go black.

"Did you think you would win against two guys three years older than you?"

He took his shirt off, groaning as the collar rubbed his face upward, his purple underwear visible above his jeans' waistline. He tossed it into the garbage. There was no way the blood and grass stains would have washed out. "It wasn't about winning." He said it in a way that implied I should have already known that. "It was about protecting you."

Yeah, I guessed my question was pretty dumb.

I was about to take care of the bloodied junk in the garbage when my brother stopped me with, "Is Felicity vicious?"

Pausing in the doorway, I looked at him over my shoulder. "No."

"*No?*"

I went down the hallway and stood on the top step when Alex's rushing feet came after me. He was still interested in City and wanted to know as much as possible about her. There was no way I could have avoided him. "Tell me about her."

I faced him fully. Would City have minded if I told him her private information?

I contemplated whether it was his business or not, which put us in an awkward moment of silence.

"There's nothing to talk about," I lied for her sake. "That's just who she is—a vicious person."

"You said she wasn't vicious."

He was cornering me and it was pressurizing.

"A family with no trust is no family at all," he said.

Actually, I didn't think it was just about wanting to know interesting little details about her. I believed he was becoming very inquisitive about the life and characteristics of my friend, and not in a good way.

Still considering it not my place to speak of her, I descended the stairs, feeling some guilt for leaving Alex in the shadows. And he still followed, not giving up. He trailed a couple of feet behind to the kitchen. I took the shirt out of the garbage can before dumping the bloodied paper towels in the other garbage can below the sink.

"Please tell me," he pleaded. That time, he sounded alarmed. Now I was sure he was nervous about this secret I was keeping from him. The fact I was hiding it meant it wasn't good. He knew that. "It's not like I'm going to run my mouth off."

"I know," I sighed from the intense pressure. I figured the only way to get him to stop nagging was to tell him everything. I turned to him once more to lay out City's life—

Bleep.

My text ringtone sounded. A blessing. I went to the table, where it lay, and looked at my lock screen. 12123 Coko St. This had been sent twenty minutes ago.

"What is it?"

"City texted me this." I suddenly had a bad feeling about it. I grabbed my car keys, heart pounding, and ran out to my car. And, of course, I was being followed.

"I'll be back soon."

"Is she okay?" he panicked.

"How should I know?"

I searched up the address on my phone. The house was located about fifteen minutes from the school.

"Should I call the police?"

I got into my car. Through the open window, I said, "No." I drove out through the gates and went to where I assumed was City's house.

I pulled into the empty driveway, trying to be calm, though I was far from it. I exited my car and looked at the brown and white house. I was feeling nauseated with nerves. I walked cautiously to the door and knocked. "City?" I asked loud enough that she might have been able to hear me from the other side.

No one came.

I knocked harder and called louder, "City."

Nothing.

Trespassing was the only other option. I turned the doorknob. The door was unlocked, making this whole thing really creepy. I opened the door and called, "City?"

It was a nice place.

I scavenged the first floor, finding nobody. I went up the stairs… and that was when time had seemed to stop. In her bedroom, City was lying on the floor unconscious, with her upper body midair, and a knife was in contact with her throat.

My heart pinched. Blood oozed out of the corner of my mouth. The demon was holding City, plus the weapon.

"Please," I said calmly, "don't hurt her."

There was no change in the knife's position.

"I'm here now," I went on, trying to soothe the ghost's intent of murdering her. "I'm here now."

Tears welled as I figured I had to take City back myself, seeming as if the ghost wasn't going to hand her over. So, I took a slow step after another slow step, approaching with extreme caution. I guessed I had gone into shock, then; everything seemed calm and my heart didn't pound the way it did a second ago. With each step, the pinch was harder and the blood flow increased. But I didn't care. I had City's life to worry about.

All this for the ghost to know we had the power of selflessness.

I took hold of the knife's handle, ignoring the agony of my blood and heart, and threw it against the wall, scarring it. Standing over the unconscious girl, I took her hands and pulled. But the demon freak had a strong hold on her shoulders, seeing how City's shoulders were aiming downwards. We were tugging on her, shock drifting away, being replaced with anxiety. I tugged and tugged, until I won tug of war. I sat on the floor with City in my lap. I hugged her tightly and wept with relief, blood dripping on her face and neck. "Wake up, City." I shook her frantically.

What felt like fingers swept my jaw. I watched blood prints floating to City's vanity mirror. The dead freak wrote a message, coming back repetitively to collect more blood:

WELL DONE, JANESSA. FELICITY AND ALLISON
WERE THERE FOR YOU BUT I WAS WONDERING
WHERE YOU WERE. CITY HELPED PROTECT YOU
TODAY. YOU RETURNED THE FAVOUR. SHE'S ALIVE
BECAUSE OF YOU.

I wept harder. I looked down at my friend. Her dark-brown-eye-shadowed eyes remained closed. "City, wake up," I pleaded, shaking her with more force.

Besides shaking her, the only part of her body that was moving was her chest—rising and falling as she breathed.

"City! City!"

I squeezed her hand.

She still lay peacefully.

I let go of her hand and went to hit her in the face—her eyes widened and saw my hand coming and caught my wrist. I breathed with relief.

She glared up. "What...?"

"It's okay. I saved you."

City grimaced and she put a hand to her head. Her eyes went to the mirror.

A few seconds later... "Holy damn." She looked back to me, fear coating her eyes. "Thank you," she breathed heavily.

Chapter 24

Allison

Hi I texted Janessa. She called me earlier, but I couldn't find my phone until now—midnight. Sometimes we texted each other in the middle of the night.

I came back from City's place a little while ago and now I'm burning my dress.

The one you got blood on yesterday?

Yes.

Why were you at City's so late?

The demon had her.

I stared at that text.

Is she okay? I texted when I realized I was still alive.

Yes she's fine.

Good, how about you?

I had internal bleeding as usual but I'm okay.

Honestly, I didn't want to know what went on at City's house. I ended the texting there, nothing more needing to know. I put my phone down on the small round glass table and propped myself up on the iron railing of the balcony. Gripping it, I gazed up at the blanket of stars.

Ghost Girl must have died a psychopath if she went as far as to torturing strangers. It would have made more sense if she attacked people she already knew. I felt sick with death images in my head. Sickness of fear of death was becoming normal to me. Maybe after it had all ended, when the job was done and we never heard from Ghost Girl again, there may be no recovery.

With City nearly dead today and Janessa always in close range, I might as well have expected something to happen to me soon—

Chapter 25

Allison

This was exactly what happened to City: Ghost Girl gave a bonk on the head and made me the prime subject of another Janessa Rescue Mission.

I could feel my eyes were open, but all I saw was black. I knew where I was. My back hurt from lying on cold stone. It was ice to my whole body. I stood up and hugged myself, building some warmth, the thin fabric of my nightgown giving none.

I knew what real terror was, so I didn't quite know what to call all *this.*

My surroundings grew more visible, and then I could make out the faint outline of the stairs. I ascended them and tried to open the door... The boxes barricaded it from the other side. I pounded my fist against the metal, having the littlest hope a live someone would hear the commotion. "Can anyone hear me?!" And there was no way of telling if it was night or day. "Hello?!"

I stopped banging to give my hand a break and gave it a shake.

"Boo!" Ghost Girl's head poked through the door.

I screamed and jumped back, forgetting about the stairs behind me and rolled down them. And I couldn't remember whether it was halfway down or right at the bottom that I felt an agonizing snap in my right elbow, but it took a moment before I realized it actually hurt. I lay on the stone floor on my left side and held my right arm. My elbow hurt like *hell.* I shouted and cried hard in pain more than fear.

Putting my chin as high as it would go, I watched Ghost Girl coming down the stairs toward me, sideways. *"I texted and called Janessa a bunch of times,"* I heard her wispy voice say over my shouting. *"She didn't get back to you."*

She texted and called Janessa? With my phone?

"I did something to my elbow," I squeezed out painfully.

She stood at my head and I rolled onto my back to look at her upside down. "How long ago?" She didn't care I might have broken my elbow.

"A few hours?" she estimated.

"Damn it," I hissed.

"She was there for Felicity," she remarked sassily, *"but she's not here now."*

"Is it the middle of the night?" I gasped through the pain. I rolled my sleeve up to take a look at my elbow. It was swollen. That was all I could tell in the darkness.

"Yeah."

"Then she's asleep."

"That's no excuse. There is no sleeping in emergencies."

"I think I screwed up my elbow," I said again. "I need the hospital."

"Janessa will take you. If she comes."

"If she doesn't?"

"You're all dead."

I didn't want to think of death, so I asked, "How did I get here?"

The dead girl looked confused. *"...I brought you here myself."*

"And no one saw an unconscious girl going down the street? All by herself? Midair?"

"I borrowed your mom's car."

"How the hell—?"

"I know how to drive."

"Allison!" a muffled voice called from the other side of the door.

Between Ghost Girl's feet, the door opened and in came my rescuer.

Chapter 26

Janessa

I flicked the switch to turn the light on, but the bulb must have burnt out. The only light in the still-very-black room was from the dimmed hallway. With it, I could see that Allison's face was of terror and pain and hope. I charged down the stairs, again having to push through my tightening heart and blood loss. I crouched next to her. "Are you okay?" I asked, beginning to help her up—

She screamed and fought out of my grip. She flopped back onto the concrete, holding her arm. "What's wrong with your arm?"

"I think my elbow is broken," she hissed. But she still got onto her feet— bare feet—without the use of her arms.

"I'm taking you to the hospital." I walked behind her with my hands on her shoulders to keep her balanced as we ascended the stairs.

Allison halted.

"What?" I asked, a little nervous the demon was blocking our way.

But Allison looked back at the floor instead, past me. She looked down there for a long time. The ghost was speaking to her.

Finally, she turned back around and said, "Let's go."

We walked briskly down the hallways in the dim light. It wasn't enough to see how her elbow looked. She wasn't bending that arm, so yes, it might have been busted.

I remembered we didn't close the basement door and barricade it. "We have to go back."

Allison was probably thinking the same thing because she snapped, "Forget the basement." Her face was of irritation, so I wasn't going to push it. The demon could close it.

A door belonging to a pair of double doors was open and we went through it and went to my car parked lousily in the parking lot. Allison looked at her elbow in the light. It was swollen and very bruised.

"Oh, my god," I said.

"Let's go!"

She startled me and I ran to the other side of my car and hopped in.

With encounters with me and the ghost came internal bleeding, so I made a habit of bringing a change of clothes everywhere I went. I reached back to Caleb's spot and snatched my vest. "Carefully put this on," I instructed, handing it to my friend.

I let her struggle with it as I hid my bloodied shirt under my black sweatshirt. Black so that blood wouldn't be visible on it and it couldn't be bloodstained. I deliberately came to Allison's rescue in black leggings and black shoes.

Driving to the hospital, I drove through stop signs—only if I saw no approaching vehicles—and sped up when traffic lights turned amber. Lucky for me, the police usually patrolled the streets on Friday nights. Not at two-fifteen in the morning on Thursdays.

While breaking the law, Allison called her mom using my phone and explained she may have had a broken elbow and that I was taking her in. But that wasn't all. She was saying things like "I can't explain that" and "Never mind" and "Just come to the hospital with my medical card," and "Bring me a pair of shoes." He mom was inquiring how the whole situation happened. Allison roared without warning and hung up. I slammed my foot on the brake. My car screeched to a stop. "What was that?" I asked in a tone saying that she could have caused an accident with her sudden shout.

"Drive."

Easing the inner tension, I put my foot on the accelerator and quickly sped up to the speed I was just at.

"She can't know why I'm out in the middle of the night, all the way uptown, with you."

"What are we going to do?"

"I… *can't* handle any questions right now."

I shut up.

The hospital was only a few minutes away now, as much time as I had to think of a plan.

And when I parked in the parking lot, decently this time, the plan was put together. Still seated, I laid it out: "This is what we're going to do: we'll stay here—right here—until your mom comes. We'll tell her you snuck out and I came to pick you up and we went back to my place—" Allison's face grew more and more anxious and confused— "and you fell on the stairs and broke your elbow and I decided to drive you to the hospital myself."

Her hazel eyes were perfect circles.

"That's all I got," I snapped at her stare.

She shook her head. "Fine. I can't top that, so let's go with it."

After waiting patiently—not patient at all, actually—Rita arrived with Joy. And given how I'd known Allison since kindergarten and our families had become super close, Allison's mom scolded both of us. "Do your maids know about this?" she shrieked.

I falsely nodded and put on a sad face.

Joy wasn't handling this very well. She was nearly in tears.

We entered the hospital, Rita quietly lecturing Allison, and Joy crushing my hand for comfort. They checked in.

Thirty minutes later— "Allison Blair?"

Allison and Rita went into the back and I stayed in the waiting room with Joy. She was *really* anxious about all this and asked, "Will Al-son b-be okay?"

I looked down at her, deliberately showing no signs of concern or worry. I squeezed her hand back, but not as hard. "She'll be fine."

"What hap-pened?"

"She fell and hurt her elbow." Well, I didn't lie. Joy was the person I hated lying to the most. I changed the subject to something uplifting. "How's school going?"

"Good."

"Do you like your teacher?"

"Yeah."

"Made any new friends?"

She shook her head, but she wasn't sad.

"I did."

"Wh-what's her name?"

"Felicity."

"Is she Al-son's fr-friend?"

I nodded with a grin.

"Al-son n-never men-tioned her."

"Oh." *Weird.*

Allison and Rita returned approximately twenty minutes later. Allison's right arm was in a cast.

Joy and I rose from the chairs, still holding hands—ever since we walked in. "So?"

"I broke it."

"Oh no."

"I'm getting surgery a week from today."

"Just be glad it's your elbow and not your head," said Rita. She was still put off this all happened.

As a group, we went back to our own vehicles. As I was beginning to hop into mine, Rita snarled, "Go straight home."

I looked past her at Allison. We were reading each other's minds: none of this was our fault.

"Are you going to school tomorrow—today?"

"Probably not."

"Okay. Take care of yourself."

Allison nodded and got into the vehicle with her mother and sister. And they drove away.

My hand was breathing heavily from being squeezed for so long. I put both hands atop the moonlit part on top of my car and put my forehead between my hands. Now *Allison* almost died. She and City were alive, but Allison didn't make it so easily. *Just be glad it's your elbow and not your head,* Rita had said.

First, I was in the hospital because of internal bleeding which no one could explain but me, then City with a knife at her throat, and now Allison with her broken elbow.

I wanted to cry, but it wasn't the time. I still had one more job to do.

I returned to the school and I cautiously walked in through the one door still open. I was solo, so if something were to happen, I wouldn't get help until the school was actually open. I walked slowly down the dim hallway, passed the classrooms, then turned another corner to the stairs hiding the basement's door. I wasn't in pain or losing any blood, so I assumed the demon wasn't present. The door was exposed. I shut it, then barricaded it with the boxes. Then I took off down the two hallways, sprinting, wanting to get there hell out of there as quickly as possible.

The lights flickered and I screamed. I felt minor pain then and the taste of copper on my tongue, but it wasn't enough of either to make me stop.

At the door, I stopped and shouted out with glances around, "Allison's safe!" I took one deep breath from sprinting. "When I'm outside, lock the doors! Otherwise it will seem like someone broke in!" Which the demon sort of did. I walked through the door hesitantly, unsure if the door would slam on me. Literally. I faced the doors. The one open slammed shut, and it made my heart leap. I could hear the lock being played with.

I bolted to my car and zoomed home, in hopes I wasn't being followed.

Chapter 27

Felicity

Entering the art room, I saw Tristan sitting across from my spot at the table all the way at the other side of the room. Was it wrong to say it bothered me? He wasn't annoying, but I felt like he was severely attracted to me, and I thought nothing of him.

I placed myself in front of him and his eyes brightened. "Hi," he said with a small smile.

I didn't return the friendliness. I wasn't the friendly type, like Smiles. "So... this is your spot now?"

His smile shriveled. "Do I annoy you? Do you want me to move?"

I didn't know how to respond. I wasn't sure what to think. I didn't know if I wanted him gone or... I didn't know what I wanted.

Tristan collected his things and stood to leave.

"No," I said all of a sudden. "Stay" escaped, too.

His smile bloomed back and he put his stuff back down.

I took *Tristan's* unicorn drawing out of my binder. All I had left to do was colour it. I eyed his box of pencil crayons and Tristan noticed. "Yes."

"Thanks."

I coloured the drawing without much thought. "What class did you just have?" Tristan asked.

"Spanish." I didn't bother looking up. And I had a feeling that he was waiting for me to ask... "And you?"

"Precalculus."

"What did Wagner do today?" It was after I asked that I looked up at him with only my eyes.

I was pretty sure his eyes were set on me ever since I got here. "Just went over the lesson." We talked about positive things, then.

This was the second time we had talked. Our conversation lasted the duration of the class. And I didn't mind it this time.

It was lunch, and as I was going to my locker, a hand on the shoulder stopped me. Smile's voice said harshly, "Basement. *Now.*"

I followed her in the opposite direction.

We pushed the boxes aside and I opened the door. I flicked the switch, but there was no light.

"The bulb burnt out," Janessa said.

Though the basement was close to black, I could see the outline of the last step, the cracks in the floor. Behind me, Janessa closed the door. Now everything disappeared. Holding my binder with one arm, I used my free hand to search blindly for my phone in my purse.

When I found it, I turned its flashlight on, and aimed it downward to light up the steps and the floor. Our footsteps echoed as we went down to the floor. I asked nervously, "Where's Allison?"

"At home." Janessa shook her head shakenly and her face aimed at the concrete. "Early this morning, the ghost brought her here, and I think it was because I came too late that the ghost did it to her—screwed up her elbow. Her elbow's broken. I saved her and took her to the hospital."

I gaped. Hell Girl injured Allison because of Janessa?

"I'm just glad she's not dead," Janessa added to my thought.

"Was her mother there?"

"Yeah. We lied about everything. We told her that Allison snuck out, I picked her up, we came back to my place, and she fell on the stairs and injured herself."

I pursed my lips and looked elsewhere.

"This is all my fault."

My eyes flicked back to Janessa. She was crouching down, breathing, "I didn't arrive in time."

I crouched before her. "But she's alive. You're doing everything right. We all are."

"How much longer will this last for?" The words were muffled by sobs.

"We may be near the end of all this torture. I mean, before the game and the task. We've all been close to meeting our fates and we saved each other from them." I put my purse and binder down and gripped her shoulders. "We'll be okay." I didn't mean to, but I spoke with a touch of softness, when I'd always spoken dryly. We sat on our knees and embraced each other. My shirt could only hold off so much of her tears before they soaked through to the skin of my shoulder.

Honestly, I was pissed. I came to a new school, a new city, for a fresh start, only to have paranormal problems with a demon from Hell stalking me and my first two decent friends ever since I lost the old ones long ago. I would have been better off continuing to commit crimes in Thumber than fighting for mine and my friends' lives against a sick ghost.

Chapter 28

Felicity

"Janessa told me what happened," I said quietly to Allison over the phone, avoiding eavesdropping.

"Yeah. Ghost Girl scared me and I fell down the stairs."

I frowned and gazed out the bus window. "She told me Hell Girl broke your elbow when she arrived to save you too late."

A pause.

"I... don't know about *that*. I mean... I was banging on the door to be let out and the ghost stuck her head through it. She scared me and I fell down the stairs backwards."

"It was a misunderstanding then." I thought about concluding it there, but a nasty thought came to mind: "Maybe Hell Girl was going to start physically breaking you anyway, and then..."

Allison's voice became dark... "Kill me and blame my death on Janessa."

Rage built slowly in the system. Janessa knew damn well what kind of problem this was and she was being too careless. Allison was always there, making her Hell Girl's favourite. I was improving on proving myself selfless. Soon Hell Girl would love me from Hell and back. Janessa...

"I don't want anything like what happened to me to happen to you or Janessa. Or something worse." Now her voice was sad.

"You and I are doing our best. Janessa can do it. Bye." I hung up without letting her say bye back.

About ten minutes later, the bus stopped, and I walked halfway down my street to my house.

A slight rumble from behind caused some curiosity. I turned my head back. A black Toyota Corolla followed, rolling at my pace. Getting a random troubling feeling, I quickened my walking, testing to see if the car's pace would increase, too. And it did.

I'd been followed on the streets before and I managed to protect myself occasionally, but I had never been followed by a vehicle before.

I didn't panic, but I broke into a run. The rumbling grew louder.

It was a challenge to run in boots that had a bit of a heel on wet concrete in the pouring rain.

I reached my house, ran up the driveway, and unlocked the door—

The car screeched to a stop. "Shitty!"

I stared forward, motionless. Only the members of the Ass Squad called me "Shitty," and I knew which of them it was. I let my purse and binder fall to my new doormat and turned around to face Will, getting out of his car and coming around to march furiously to me. I took my jacket off, preparing for what was to come next. "You hit me with the bat." He referred to today in PE; when Moretti wasn't looking, I whacked him with the bat in the stomach, finally getting revenge for him knocking me out with the baseball last week. Now he wanted payback for my payback. "Now I'm going to hit you."

"Try." I was ready. I marched toward him, and in close enough range, I pulled my fist back and swung at his face, striking his cheek, causing him to stumble backwards onto the grass. I followed. He threw his fist at my mouth, but I caught it in my palm a centimeter away. I swung again with my free hand, only to have mine in his grasp. Pushing against each other, we tried to get the other down.

My boots were sliding in the mud, making it difficult to get Will on the ground. He was winning. Until I hooked my leg around his and continued pushing.

The rain turned to waterfalls, showering us, but helping me get him down on his back. Will slipped and tripped and fell onto his back. I let myself fall on him and my kneecap pounded his gut. He grunted and threw his fist up, getting my mouth, cutting my lip on the inside—knowing that from the taste of blood. He struck me again, in the nose, and then the cheek.

Knees on each side of his body, I glared down at him and smashed his face. My fist was wet with blood and rain.

About to hit him again, I came to terms with myself and realized I beat him bad enough. After a hundred blows to the face, he was too weak to fight. I was breathing through my mouth, my lip throbbing, blood trickling over and down. The blood from my nose fell on Will's face. My cheek hurt like hell. I stood up, keeping my eyes on the dumbass between my boots. "You followed me all the way here for *this*?"

He peered through his swollen eyelids, the little of his eyes seen filled with pissiness. He shifted onto his bottom and I kindly backed off to let him pick himself up. He stalked to his car, bellowing back, "GO TO HELL!"

I did and said nothing.

He zoomed away.

When the rumbling of his car faded with distance, I went inside to clean myself up. My white leggings were muddy on the knees, so muddy it would be impossible to get the brown off. For now, I put my sodden clothes on the bathroom's countertop and showered.

I put on my fuzzy dark pink nightgown from the night before. I threw my leggings out, put my shirt in the laundry, and wiped my boots clean with Lysol wipes.

I sat in front of the TV and iced my cheek. There would be a bruise by the following day and probably last for the week. Possibly an ugly one.

I just hoped desperately Hell Girl was with either Allison or Janessa during that time. If she saw me fight alone, that would have endangered the girls. Not that I needed them, but still, she would brutally punish them. However, there were no signs of her being around, including how I didn't hear her.

It took a little over two hours to complete my homework: reading the first two pages of that homeostasis booklet, studying for a geography quiz which was on Tuesday, and working on my oral presentation for Spanish based on a short story we read.

I didn't know how the girls felt—probably the same. It was hard to focus on school with a psychotic ghost after us. I got a B- on a Spanish quiz that wasn't meant to be hard to study for.

"How was work?" I asked Dad as he came into the kitchen.

I had ordered pepperoni pizza and was onto my third slice.

"Good. A vicious Pomeranian chomped on my hand though." He showed me the teeth marks, indented between his thumb and index finger.

"Is Ravendale Animal Hospital better than Thumber Animal Clinic?"

His green eyes widened as he bit into a slice. "Mm-hmm."

"What makes it better?"

"The coworkers. By far."

I didn't care about any of this, but just to be respectful to my father, I acted like I did.

"What have you done to your face?"

Though he asked all of a sudden, I wasn't the least startled. "Fight."

"At school?"

"The guy followed me home."

"What?"

Why was he so alarmed? He knew I could handle myself. For the most part. "Don't call the police. I took care of him." To prevent the conversation from going any further, I went up to my room.

Chapter 29

Allison

This was the third day of having a broken elbow, and it sucked. I missed two days of school and I couldn't go to soccer practice.

Mom was working and Joy was spending the day with Molly, so I was spending mine with Roman. Every Saturday, he would watch me play, but since I had an injury, he came over instead.

I lay on his lap, my left hand on top of my right, with one of his atop and his elbow supporting my head. We watched *The Terminator*, but it was sideways in my view. "I can't stand this," he mumbled.

I smiled and looked up at him. Feeling the movement, he looked down at me, his dark eyes simply miserable. "Well," I stated in a playful commanding way, "I'm hurt, and until I'm back to normal, I call the shots."

"Damn you" was spoken as a joke.

I loved the *Terminator* movies, but this guy didn't like them. Roman liked things that were more realistic. Not a bunch of cyborgs trying to kill each other.

I looked back to the TV, but my mind was elsewhere. "I wish I went to school the last two days. It's going to be tough to catch up on missing work. And I wish I was at soccer right now. I need it for school."

"For *school?*"

"I didn't have room on my schedule for PE, so I'm doing it online. It's a good idea to take PE to become a homicide detective."

"What...?"

"Right now, I'm focusing on ten courses to become a homicide detective. I'm taking one online and the other I'm going to take in summer school."

"What are you taking *now*? Biology, physics, English..."

"...Spanish, calculus, sociology, chemistry, and computers."

"What will you take in summer school?"

"Psychology."

"Wow," he said in bewilderment. "Are you managing?"

I sighed, "Yes and no. Physics, English, biology, and Spanish are really easy. Sociology and chemistry are *okay*. And calculus and computers are complicated."

"I'm just taking easy classes."

"Easy year for you."

The subject was replaced with one I *really* wouldn't have expected: "Who's that blonde friend of yours? Felicity?" Roman never really inquired about girls.

"Felicity Hale," I answered in way that wouldn't make his unexpected question seem unexpected.

"New?"

"From Thumber."

"She's got a bit of a dark side, doesn't she?"

Again, I looked up at his face, already down at me. How many people saw that fight? Everyone? "A dark side? She's all dark."

"She's like... the school celebrity. More and more people know who she is." Roman went on to justifying his statement. "*No one* stood up to them before, as stupid as that may be. Maisie thinks she controls the school like a queen, and given how vicious the other members of her group are, the school's scared to mess with them. And then, one day, Felicity came along, not afraid of being beaten up or whatever."

"Well, Will got her back by knocking her out with a baseball in PE." His eyes narrowed in discomfort.

My eyebrows rose. "Yeah, I know. But City wasn't the least concerned about it. I'm not kidding. Anyone who screws with her..."

"Why is she like this? Nobody is *just like this*."

Honestly, it wasn't my business to discuss City's life with anyone. Even with herself. At the same time, Roman and I never kept secrets from one another. I wasn't going to lie, either. I either told him the truth or I said nothing at all. Not knowing what to say or do, I turned back to the TV, sheepishly.

"Not my business?" he asked in a tone that described him being cool. "I accept that."

But I wasn't cool. Without turning back, I said, "She's from the dark side of this world." I felt horrible for saying it, but if I were to say that City was happy as hell and full of light, I would have felt worse, and he would have known it was a lie. *Nobody is just like this,* he had said. Sometimes the truth wasn't pretty. "But her life wasn't always full of darkness. Her mother died some years back and her life turned upside down. She was twelve or thirteen. I don't remember the exact age. Who she is now is the opposite of who she was."

"Wow."

I turned back then to see Roman's eyes turn glossy. Sometimes he could be a little emotional.

Our voices turned sad as the talk escalated. "When she first told me and Janessa about it, I felt broken. She's my friend, so I felt the loss, too."

"You have suffered the loss of a loved one before."

"My dad's not dead."

"But he's gone, right?"

A tear slipped down my temple. Roman picked up my good hand and brought it up to his mouth. "I'm so sorry," he breathed, and hissed it.

"I feel bad for Joy more than myself," I said truthfully.

"Let's just watch the movie," he said firmly, to put aside the negativity.

Hopefully City could find a way out of the dark. But I believed she was in the best place to recover from all the trauma of the past.

Chapter 30

Janessa

The demon harassed me ever since Thursday—starting in the middle of the night.

I thought I left her behind at school, but she followed me home.

City, Allison, and I had to prove ourselves a little bit more. And then the game would begin. The demon said I was lucky Allison didn't die that night, and she was proud of my remarkable improvement. How did I know all this? I asked the questions aloud and the demon wrote the answers in blood. It took a lot of blood to do it. And it took an hour to scrub the outside wall of my mansion clean. All this happened yesterday. The boys had hockey practice and Denise went with them, Kira went grocery shopping, and Malia took a long nap. I was left unattended, giving the demon the advantage.

This morning, I woke with a dry red line from the corner of my mouth to my earlobe. But throughout the day, I lost none. Throughout the day, I feared that by the end of *all this*, I had lost every drop of blood in my body. I would be nothing but a white, bony corpse. Though the demon had said I had to live for Allison and City, just as they had to live for me, I had the slightest thought it was all a game to her, threatening and hurting us for no literal reason.

I believed the demon had left to return very soon.

"Janessa!"

I looked up from my novel and turned my head to Caleb rushing in. When he was close enough, I saw a gap in his toothy smile. I scooched to sit on the edge of my bed and he stood before me. He opened his fist and the missing tooth lay in his palm. "I lost my tooth!" he exclaimed.

I smiled and said sweetly, "Tonight you have to put it under your pillow for the tooth fairy."

Caleb was a strong believer in the tooth fairy, Santa, the Easter Bunny, and the Grim Reaper. Obviously he didn't know, but I was his tooth fairy. I flushed his teeth down the toilet and left a quarter under his pillow every time he lost a tooth.

And this was why he believed in the Grim Reaper: he went trick-or-treating with Joy when he was three and she was seven and walking up a driveway, a toy Grim Reaper sensed their motions and it "came to life" and scared them away. They took off down the street, in an unknown neighbourhood, and Denise had to run after them. So, for the future Halloweens, Joy and Caleb dressed up at super-heroes, thinking they would fight the Grim Reaper one day. But Joy was ten now and knew that it was fake, but dressed like a superhero with Caleb for his sake.

"I'll put it there now!" He turned and ran.

And I went back to reading, though homework was always my first prior-ity. With the demon attacking me, City, and Allison, school was practically impossible. Motivation was in surviving, not schooling.

Suddenly not feeling the mood to read anymore, I put my book aside—heart thumping a little harder than normal—and began working on the dress I started putting together back in the summer. Well, it was just the top. The skirt I hadn't gotten to yet. The top was navy blue with thin straps and a V-neck. I lay it on my desk and took a seat. I opened the top drawer—heartbeat quickening—and took out a Ziplock bag with mini square pieces of fabric.

My fingers shook as I held a dark pink square with a thumb and an index finger, and it was difficult to steady the scissors as I cut it into petals. At this point, inside my ribcage was thunderous, and it was all because of constant nerves. I had to breathe through my mouth. I had no control over my thoughts and fear. Images of City's and Allison's attacks overpowered me when I should have been overpowering them.

I cut right through the petal. Not wanting to screw up on any more petals, I put the fabric and scissors down and jumped up from my chair. I walked wall to wall, nauseated.

Suddenly needing fresh air, I threw the glass door open and stepped onto the balcony. There was no telling whether I was going to erupt or not, but just to avoid any splashes on the marble, I leaned over the railing, panting uncontrollably.

I waited for roughly a minute to let the stomach juice rush like a river up my esophagus and out like a waterfall… but nothing happened.

My legs giving up on me, I sank to the marble, crying wildly, but still trying to not make so much commotion, and leaned back against the railing. I hugged a knee already tucked in. I dipped my chin and sobbed like hell.

I wanted the ghost gone. *Gone.* Back to Hell. The normal life ended. The new life began in the first week of school. The life of paranormality. The life of fear. The life of hell. The life of death. But at least I wasn't left to stand alone. I just wished I could seek support from my brothers and maids. But that would have created two problems: jeopardizing mine, City's, and Allison's lives, and making myself look like a psych job and be taken to see a professional in abnormal behaviour of fear of the dead.

When I managed to collect myself, I rose and went back inside, giving myself a comforting hug. I left the glass door open for the fresh air my mind desperately needed… only to feel like fainting. On the wall above my desk was a message written in washable marker. I couldn't read it from this angle, so I moved positions:

READY FOR ROUND THREE?

Chapter 31

Felicity

My eyes flared open as soon as I regained consciousness, which I didn't know how I lost in the first place. I lay underneath the fuchsia sunset. I went to sit upright—I felt something sharp poke the sides of my hands. The pokes wanted to keep me down. Immediately I knew Hell Girl set up another Save Felicity Mission. Was this a game to her? Maybe.

Panic circulated alongside the rush of blood. I felt sick, like throwing-up sick.

Moving my head about, I examined my surroundings… the school… I lay on the field… dirt-covered knives poked my skin.

"Janessa and Allison should be here any minute now."

"You ass," I growled.

Now the knives pierced my hands, drawing a little blood. I grimaced.

"How did I get here?" I made my voice calm to avoid pissing her off anymore.

"I brought you here."

"And no one noticed a body being dragged on the street?" I looked down my body to my legs and turned them. My pants had some tears and spots of dirt.

"Not when I don't want them to. But for getting Allison here, I borrowed her mom's car. She lives too far away to drag all the way here."

I blinked. "You can drive?"

"Felicity!"

I tilted my head back to see Janessa and Allison running upside down. The closer Janessa came, the more blood that dripped from her mouth. They stared horridly at me, the position I was in, and Hell Girl explained, *"Janessa has to take the knives away from Felicity's hands. But just to warn you, the pain and blood loss will be excruciating, probably to the point where she'll abandon Felicity, who is at the risk of sepsis."*

A break in speech so Allison could repeat it for Janessa, whose eyes reddened.

"Allison"—Allison looked from Janessa back to Hell Girl— *"you have to forcefully push her."*

Allison repeated that.

"If you take too long, I'll cut her wrists, too, increasing the risk."

I glared up at the sky, trying to force the anger and terror out by finding peace with the beauty above.

The knives deepened into my skin and my grimace was the signal to begin. Allison put herself behind Janessa and shoved her forward. At first, Janessa went willingly, but drawing nearer and nearer, she was more resistant.

Millimeter by millimeter, the knives made their way to the other side of my palms, digging deeper and deeper.

Janessa was crying out and clutching her stomach with an arm, and her hand went to her mouth, trying to keep her blood inside her. Blood leaked through her thumb and upper lip and her pinkie and chin.

"Go!" Allison barked, pushing harder.

Dark lines engraved my palms from one side to the other, as dark as red wine. The knives floated to my wrists and the points pierced them. I hissed ferociously. It was in that moment that I no longer heard wails and shouts. Everything turned calm, quiet. The sky verified that Smiles was too good of a person to be tortured for someone like me—a troubled girl with no life, nothing to live for. And this was a test of selflessness, right? I didn't want to die, but if this was my new life, then there was no damn way I wanted to live through it. Besides, I would reunite with Mom.

Noise returned to the world around me, and I screamed so loud it hurt my lungs, "STOP!"

My friends shut up. The knives—they cut three inches of my wrists up toward the crooks of my arms—stopped, too.

"Stop… torturing yourselves." My voice had a raspy tone. "Just let me—"

Janessa knew what the next word was going to be and didn't let me say it. She charged forward with a violent cry, reached down to grab the knives, and threw one right, the other left.

I gaped and shook at the sound of her cry. She collapsed at my head. I sat at her side and pulled her bloodied body onto my lap, leaving blood handprints on her arms. We shared blood. Her jaw and shirt were coated with it. Her face was blank; she was in shock. Her eyes gazed dumbly at the fuchsia. I looked up, too, relieved I was alive.

"Tell her well done for me."

I glared at Allison, who glared at Hell Girl. "Forget her," I snapped. "I need the hospital."

Allison looked down to me. "Yeah," she said shakily, nodding.

"Let's go."

We looked down at Janessa, who was immediately coming out of shock. "Are you okay to drive?" Allison asked, worrisome.

"Yeah, I'm okay." Smiles sat upright and got to her feet. We—wasn't sure about Hell Girl—went to her car. Touching the door, I left a blood handprint, appearing slightly purple on the blue. I didn't care about the seatbelt. I wanted my cuts to be cleaned and stitched.

Sepsis followed untreated blood poisoning. Did Hell Girl know that? Or was that exaggerated, threatening Janessa and Allison into hurrying up? It would have made more sense that it was completely exaggerated, intending to scare them.

Chapter 32

Allison

I took my phone out of my purse and asked, "City, what's your dad's number?" I looked back at her. She folded her bloodied hands and pressed her wrists together to help ease the blood. She gave me the number.

"Hello?" asked a really deep voice.

"Mr. Hale?"

"Yes?"

"This is Allison. I'm with Felicity. We're going to the hospital. She's badly hurt."

"I'm on my way."

"Okay." We hung up. "He's going to meet us there," I said to City as I put my phone back in my purse.

She was silent.

At the hospital, I helped City out. We took some steps to the entrance before I stopped and spun around. "Aren't you coming?"

"My face," Janessa snapped.

"Just go home," said City. "Allison's going to help me."

I spun back around. "How will I get home?"

"My dad and I will take you."

Back to Janessa: she nodded. "Okay. Bye. Take care of yourselves."

"Bye," mine and City's voices overlapped.

Janessa drove off into the purple of the occuring night.

City and I went inside to the front desk, walking briskly. "I need to be seen now." City wasn't being the least polite.

The secretary gaped at her blood-caked hands.

Drip, drip, drip.

I looked down and blood drops dripped onto the floor between City's shoes. I looked back in the direction we came from. She left a trail of them.

"Come," the secretary said in a European accent.

City followed her and I followed City. And as if the secretary sensed it, she looked back over her shoulder. "Unfortunately, you can't come. Please wait in the waiting room."

City ignored how I went the opposite way as instructed. I went through the double doors and took a seat.

A man walked up to the desk. I sort of forgot what City's father looked like, so I slightly figured it was him, but then I was a hundred percent sure he was when he asked, "Is there a girl named Felicity Hale here?" he asked the secretary's momentarily replacement.

I rushed to him. But he was too panicked to see me at his side.

"Well," the replacement started, "a blonde girl came in with severe cuts on her hands and wrists. That could be her."

"That *is* her," I said to both of them. The man looked down at me. To the replica of City's green eyes, I said, "Felicity went to get her hands bandaged or stitched."

He nodded, acknowledging me.

"Is she your daughter?"

"Yeah," he said to the replacement.

"Do you have her medical card?"

He put it on the counter.

When the replacement was finished with it, he handed it back to Mr. Hale. "The nurse will come speak with you shortly. Please be seated in the waiting room."

"Thank you," my friend's dad and I said, voices overlapping. He turned to me then and we walked together. "What happened?" he demanded. He was almost like the adult male version of City with his harshness and eyes. The only differences were the curly hair and style of speaking—no dryness.

"She can explain it better than me," I said hesitantly. City would have had the perfect lie. I wanted to let her figure out how to explain the cuts.

Mr. Hale scoffed, but he accepted it. What a relief.

"Adam Hale?"

Though I was rejected before, I rose with Mr. Hale and followed him and the nurse down several hallways. I guessed that time I was accepted. We came to a room with City sitting on the bed and a cart of medical supplies next to her. A doctor was there, too.

Unlike City, I followed rules. I knew it wasn't all my business to know the conditions she was under, but she was my friend. I stood behind the wall, out of sight, though she already saw me, but didn't give me away. She only said, "Hi" to her dad.

"Sweetie, are you alright?"

"She has four deep cuts: two on her hands and two on her wrists. She shouldn't have any infections as long as she keeps her hands and wrists dry and bandaged for at least forty-eight hours. She should come back in five days for me to see how well her wounds have healed, and if we can, we'll remove her stitches."

I felt a hundred times better.

"I cleaned her cuts thoroughly," the doctor added.

That put me at ease. City was going to be fine.

"Can she go to school?"

"Yes, but not PE. I already told her this."

Mr. Hale said nothing to that.

"Make an appointment for her to get her stitches checked."

"I'll do that."

Mr. Hale and the doctor exited the room and didn't notice me; they went the other way. I walked in. Her hands and wrists were wrapped in several layers of bandages. I was a mix of happy and sad. "I'm glad you're okay," I said softly.

"So am I." City was a little groggy.

"Did you get surgery?"

"Minor surgery. I shouldn't get *sepsis* now."

I nodded, though she would have to get blood poisoning first. I felt that sepsis threat was exaggerated, looking back at that. Ghost Girl might have just been trying to get into mine and Janessa's heads. But there was an extremely high probability that she was going to be fine. I figured it was safe to say she was going to be fine. We fell quiet for a few minutes, and I was sitting on the chair.

City broke the silence with, "On Monday, we're meeting in the basement. Text Janessa."

"Okay."

Her father returned. "Let's go."

With my good hand, I helped City down from the bed, though maybe she didn't need it, but appreciated the help. "She needs a ride home," City said.

His eyes flicked to me. "Where do you live?"

"Downtown."

His eyes widened. Downtown was a forty-five minute drive away. But he went along with it. "Okay."

City and I didn't talk to each other for the entire drive. She was telling her father a story about how she got her cuts: she had a rage attack, smashed a glass cup, went to get a broom and dustpan, and dumbly fell on the shards. He thought it was sketchy, but didn't question it. For example, what was my involvement in all this? The only thing he cared about was his daughter's safety.

They also went through the instructions on how to care for her wounds, as a reminder. He pulled up in front of my apartment, and I said, "Have a good night" to both of them. Mr. Hale returned it, but City didn't. She gave me a reminding glare that we were meeting in the basement on Monday. Why we were going to the basement, I didn't know.

Chapter 33

Janessa

I entered my history classroom, my anxiousness reaching the sky; Maisie and Cody watched intently as I went to my desk. But this was much better than the demon attacks. Even as I just sat there, I felt their hateful eyes on me from the other side of the room.

Most of the students—in all classes—tried to sit as far away from them as possible. In this class, five were unlucky.

I tried to look straight ahead and simply ignore them, but my eyes wanted to go for their direction and I couldn't stop them. I accidently gave in. "Is there a problem?" I asked calmly.

The students who had already arrived watched us. The ones coming in didn't pay too much attention.

Maisie's eyes widened, but she kept silent. As did Cody's. They weren't prepared for me to speak up "without their permission." Again.

"Don't mind them."

My focus turned on a girl a named Kennedy. She usually sat in the back, alone, but I guessed she decided to claim the desk beside mine. I loved her hair, and always had; it was dyed copper red and it was styled differently each day. Today it was in a waterfall braid.

The tension in the class died slowly.

The second bell went and Mr. Astafei walked in and started class. "Okay," he began, taking his seat at his desk before the class. He lowered his glasses over his eyes. Placing a copy of our homework under the overhead, he continued in his Romanian accent with, "Take out your homework."

Paper shuffled as we did.

Mr. Astafei read out the first question: "When did World War 1 begin?"

"July 28, 1914," I called out.

He nodded and wrote it in purple ink, allowing everyone to see the answer.

Calling out the answer allowed me to contain some focus on school instead of Maisie and Cody and the demon, though it was a battle between me and the demon attacks, always on mental replay. Kennedy was slight protection from the loser squad and Allison and City were strong protection from the dead girl. But, of course, the ghost was the deadlier issue.

I guessed I could have seen this coming: I got all the answers wrong except the first. The demon was screwing up my marks, and by the end of this term, my grades would be so low that it would be so hard to get them up.

Biology class was next.

City walked in just as the second bell sounded. Her hands were bandaged and it seemed to ascend further up her arm, but both sides were concealed by her sleeves. And she looked really pretty with her hair up in a bun. "Felicity."

She, Allison, and I turned to Tristan, waving her over to him, plus his four friends. She obeyed. She crossed her arms on his and his friend's table. "Did you get twenty-four?" Tristan referred to the homework.

City looked down and read the question. "The cell membrane gives the cell its shape and protection and controls movement of substances in and out of the cell."

"Thanks."

She nodded and sat with me and Allison.

For the duration of class, we did in-class work based on cell structure and function and homeostasis. My friends and I did the first few questions before stopping. Mr. Wilson being the easy-going teacher he was, he let his students do whatever they wanted once he discussed the lesson and the assignment. But, of course, he preferred if everyone used their class time wisely. For our own sake. I stopped because my thoughts had finally claimed the victory. City? Allison? I could only assume it was for the same reason.

"We're going to the basement at lunch," City quietly reminded us.

"Will *she* be there?" I asked in the same volume as City. "Do you know?"

"I don't know."

No problem. I didn't want to know anyway.

Half an hour later was lunch. City, Allison, and I went to the basement, discreetly. We unbarricaded the door and I opened it and led them into the blackness. City, the last in, closed the door. We turned our phone's flashlights on to light our way down the steps. City and I sat on the last step and Allison stood before us, holding the hand of her injured arm with the hand of the good one. "It's almost over—this torturing shit," City hissed, her hiss echoing a bit. "We're making it."

Hers and Allison's faces changed. "So, she came," Allison told me.

"Great," City said, vexed. "Let's play your fucking game."

My way of following the conversation was by listening to what the girls had to say. Allison asked, "What's the game?"

A pause. The girls eyed each other and me.

The pause was carrying on for a long while.

The demon pissed City off, given how her eyes raged with green fire and she turned a lot more intimidating than normal. "Damn it!" she said harshly.

Silence again, but Allison's eyes followed the invisible being up the steps. "So, that's it? Just unt—"

A sudden pause.

"*Crap,*" said City dramatically.

Another break in speech.

"For who?" City asked the ghost, eyes looking to the door.

Pause.

"You won't tell me? You just want me to find a *good therapist*? What the hell?"

Pause.

"This isn't making any sense."

"She's gone," Allison told us. "*For now.*"

"Well...?" I asked.

City let Allison do the informing. "We pleased her. Now Ghost Girl has to set up the game for us to play. It's going to take some time, so in the meantime, we focus on getting our grades up. She presumes we're failing our classes due to all the terrorizing. And she thanks us for torturing ourselves for her."

City's eyes still maintained their fieriness. The gratitude from the ghost must have been what threw her off so much.

"She still wants us to take care of each other, though," Allison added, "for the game and the task."

"Makes sense," I said.

We sat in peaceful silence. I thought of all the blood I lost and the terror I endured for the lives of my friends. None of us had it easy; I had sequences of internal bleeding in the demon's presence, Allison had a broken elbow, and City's hands and wrists were sliced open, and the scars would give her clear memory of all this hell. Two more periods of Hell Time before it came to a completed end. Except the fear may last forever.

"So, what now?" I asked.

"Our lives resume, and when the time comes for us to play the game, we'll be ready. We've survived proving ourselves, which I believed we would, so I'm almost positive we'll survive the game."

"What do you mean 'almost?'" Allison looked freaked out.

City explained: "We don't know what the game is, so there's no telling what we're in for. However, we weren't prepared for all the bad shit we went through and we're alive."

Allison and I looked at each other, and City added, "Let's try to keep it that way."

For my last two classes—English and art—I managed to keep more focus than before on my tasks. Knowing the haunting hadn't come to an end left me with a great deal of anxiety. At least the girls and I had a break. But how long it would be was unknown. Maybe a week or two?

Not giving it much thought, I wanted to know what the demon's motive was. I wanted to know what the game was, what the task was. Did they involve more harm and near-death situations? Or was there going to be a new requirement? A new rule? I had many questions, but the demon had gone off somewhere to prepare the game. It wasn't like she would give me straight answers anyway.

Honestly, all I could do now was just concentrate on school, continue to protect my friends, "prove" to my family there was *absolutely nothing wrong with me,* and pay the ghost no mind until the game began, like what City and Allison said.

Chapter 34

Felicity

"Let's see."

I sat on the chair and stuck out my arms for Doctor Bryant, the doctor from five days ago. He had to inspect my stitches for any infections. "No redness," he observed. "Let's remove them." With tweezers and scissors, he carefully tugged the threads out of my flesh and cut them off. I was left with four pink scars that would turn white at some point.

I had five very visible scars on my body, one in which was concealed with dark lipstick and a lip ring.

Doctor Bryant put medical tape on my new scars and gave instructions on how to care for them.

I thanked him and returned to Dad.

"So?" Dad stood from a chair in the waiting room.

My reply was, "I have to do this and that, this and that, and that and this."

Pulling into the driveway, something yellow on the door caught my attention. Something black was scribbled on it, but was blurry with the too-far distance. I wanted to get there before Dad, so I threw the door open a few seconds before the truck stopped and quickly got out. Without making it seem obvious, I casually speed-walked to the door. I peeled the sticky note off and read "MEETS US IN RAVENDALE PARK AT MIDNIGHT" in sloppy writing.

Cody wrote this. I didn't know what was going to go down tonight. I didn't know who would all be there. Maybe just the members of the Ass Squad. I was going for two reasons: I was always in the mood for beating their asses and this might have had something to do with Janessa or Allison. The Ass Squad was a threat to us. And before Hell Girl vanished, she told us to keep watching each other's backs. For safety reasons, I wasn't going to disappoint.

"Is something wrong?"

"No." I opened the door and went up to my room. Now that I was in a private room, I searched up directions to Ravendale Park. It was going to be a dangerous walk; an hour in the dark night alone, there and back. The last time I wandered through the streets at night solo, I received a cut on the lip, which wasn't *terrible*, and it could have been worse.

Tonight, I would bring my phone and a knife taped to my back. I would use the knife to scare off anyone who considered to attack me just by pulling it out, showcasing it. If that failed, then I would make small cuts, as many as necessary.

I was going to sneak out at eleven and get home as soon as possible. And hopefully, Dad wouldn't wake at any point while I was gone.

At a quarter to eleven, I quietly and slowly opened Dad's bedroom door ajar. Based on the silhouette against the dark of the room, he was asleep. I went back to my room and changed into black clothing. I put my hair back in a po nytail. I didn't bother with makeup or my lip ring. I put my phone in my leather jacket's pocket and descended the stairs slow as an old dog trying to get to places. I had to avoid my high-heel boots making clicking sounds. In the kitchen, I took a knife with a five-inch blade from the knife holder, opened a drawer that contained duct tape, and placed them on the countertop. It took a few seconds to lift my shirt up at the back and hold it there with one hand. One-handedly, I duct taped the knife to my lower back, and let my shirt and jacket fall over it.

Then I went out the door and locked it.

Under the street lights, I walked at a normal pace.

Street after street, the night was peaceful, unlike Thumber's nights, when troubled teens were out to play. I was entering further into the unknown areas, occasionally watching my surroundings.

About forty-five minutes later, I was at the bottom of a massive hill, just past another unknown neighbourhood. Ravendale Park was on the other side, approximately ten minutes away once I travelled over the hill. Staying to the side, I walked over it, and going down, my legs quickened to a near-run due to the steepness.

There was a final neighbourhood I had to walk through. Just past it would be the park.

Forty feet away from the neighbourhood, I walked in through the park's gate. I was kind of impressed by what the park had: a baseball diamond, two sets of goalposts for soccer and football, a huge playground, and a massive waterpark within. Thumber's parks were nothing like this. I would have loved this when I was little.

Past the playground stood six shadowed figures. I mentally prepared myself for the worst as I calmly walked up to them. And when close enough, they saw me approaching. I felt lured in.

Maybe ten feet away, I stopped in my tracks. "Let's make this quick. What do you want?"

"We want you *gone*," Ass Leader snarled.

"As in dead?"

"That would be better."

I smirked. "I'm here to stay."

Cody...? stalked toward me and I knew what was coming. He threw a fist at my face, but like the first time, I caught it with a *clap*. "Stop trying," I said in a way to make him feel stupid. From there, he tried to flip me onto the ground with hits and misses. I fought back. Just as I was about to hook a leg around his, a second set of hands gripped my shoulders and pulled me backwards. It was too all of a sudden for me to defend myself, so getting me on my back was easy. Will stood over me and stomped on my hands and kept them on the grass, just long enough for Cody to regather himself and planted his shoe in my stomach with such force. I wanted to clutch my stomach as I gasped for air, but my hands were caught between shoes and grass.

"You see?" Maisie asked annoyedly. "This is what happens when you misbehave." She said that part in a bit a baby tone.

"What the hell is your problem?" I wheezed.

"You ruined my life."

"Your life?" What a psychopath. "You don't have one."

"Life is all about taking what you want using fear and violence. That's how I get what I want. That's why no one fucks with me." The psychopath crouched down next to me and tilted her head to the side. Her voice was soft with danger. "But you don't seem to be scared of anything."

The events with Hell Girl ran in circles in my head, but of course I didn't mention that weakness. I just said, "Certainly not you." Maybe I should have been scared of her and her squad. They had issues. *Serious issues.*

I regained my breath. I had the energy to get myself out of here. I kicked my legs up and over my head to kick Will's knees. He stumbled back. And then I side-kicked Maisie to make sure she wouldn't do anything to keep me down. She rolled onto her back, and before Will and Cody were on top of me, I reached under my back and ripped the knife off it. I sliced Cody's hands in less than a second, which were going for my shoulders. He hissed and backed off. I flipped around and got into a sitting position face to face with Will. I cut his face from beside his nose to his ear. I was supposed to make small cuts, but... I had the knife in my attacking position, warning everyone to stay the hell back. Will put a hand to his face, the other to the air, and backed off slowly, silently telling me he wasn't a threat anymore. I snapped my head back, just in time to see that Cody was going to jump onto me but decided against it.

I stood up, knife still raised. I took a long moment to look at each member of the Ass Squad. "You should all know by now I'm not someone *you* want to fuck with," I said in a death-warning tone, returning the psychopathy. "You'll stay away from me, you'll stay away from Janessa, and you'll stay away from Allison." I had a sudden thought. "And Alex."

"Who Alex?" Cody asked.

"That boy you and Will beat up not that long ago. Anyway, stay away from us, or you'll get hurt, and I'm not afraid of killing you if I seriously have to." Obviously, I didn't mean it, although saying it may have been the only way to protect myself, Janessa, Allison, and Alex. The volume of my voice increased by a lot when I asked, *"Do you understand!"*

They nodded.

Feeling that I'd ended the conflict between the ten of us, I turned and left the park. Exiting the gate, I slid the knife up my sleeve to keep it hidden.

Coming to think of it, I was glad all that happened. Hell Girl would have been very glad to hear that I was "willing to sacrifice a group of shitheads so that they would stop harassing us and we would be safe." From them.

Chapter 35

Allison

I missed school for my operation. It should have been done yesterday, but someone was literally dying and needed immediate medical attention.

I was greeted by a nurse. "Hello," she said.

I returned her greeting and followed her to a room where I needed to put on a gown.

After, I was questioned about my medical history. All I really had to say was that I was healthy and that the only medication I was taking at the moment was what the doctor prescribed to me for my injury.

Next was checking my heart rate, body temperature, blood pressure, and pulse, talking me through the steps. "I'm going to swab your arm and put an IV line in," Doctor Bryant said, putting a disinfectant substance on a cotton ball. He swept my arm with the cotton ball before gently poking a needle in my vein.

Then I was wheeled on a hospital wheel bed into the operating theater. Doctor Bryant said, "I'm going to cut your cast off," and with a cast saw, he cut through it.

Once it was off, the anesthesiologist gave me general anesthetics. Then a mask was placed over my mouth…

My eyes opened a bit and I was looking up at a familiar ceiling. Bit by bit, I was awakening. With the bit of strength I found, I looked at my arm. Again, in a cast. I felt drowsy and couldn't comprehend where I was. And... it was weird; I was pretty sure I woke after surgery before now.

I looked around the room without moving my head. Of course, I couldn't see much, but the little I saw made me realize I was in my room.

Joy appeared in my peripheral vision. "H-how are y-you?"

"I'm okay," I mumbled.

I woke again for dinner and walked to the kitchen like a zombie. I didn't have much appetite, though I didn't eat all day. All I was having was fries.

"Janessa and Felicity came by," said Mom, taking a sip of water.

I downed three quarters of orange juice and put my glass down and said nothing. I wasn't in the mood for a bunch of talking.

"They brought those." She gestured to something behind me and I turned slowly. A bouquet of purple and white dahlias in a glass vase sat on the counter. Dahlias were my favourite kind of flower. And leaning on the vase was a pink envelope.

I got up slowly to open it, ignoring the fact my fingers were greasy. I managed with only one hand. I read the card:

Hope you feel better soon.
Love Felicity and Janessa.

I had energy for a weak smile.

That was something Janessa and I had done for years: give each other get-well cards when we had severe illnesses or injuries. I started it when Janessa sprained her ankle badly at skating. Following that, I had a high fever and she sent me a get-well card in return.

Janessa was the sweetest person I knew. Was City sweet? I wanted to say she was, but I had absolutely no idea.

"It was really sweet of them," Mom remarked from behind, replicating my thoughts. "Is Felicity a nice girl?"

I shrugged.

"I'm sure she may be kind-hearted, but just doesn't show it much."

That was basically right.

I was willing to tell Mom about her, but again, I had no energy for speaking. At some point, I was going to tell her about City; who exactly she was, what her personality was like, where she was from, how dangerous she could be, so on.

We finished dinner and I went to sit alone on my room's balcony. Past the sounds of traffic, I thought about Ghost Girl. It was such a relief we survived the first of three parts of the haunting, but I didn't know if we would survive the next or even the one after that. I guessed the only thing to do now was pray for mine and my friends' lives. We would keep protecting each other, as Ghost Girl wanted. I wanted to be faithful, so once we made it though *all* the hell, we would return to living normally—if it was possible. Developing mental trauma that lasted until death was very probable. We just had to be even braver and stronger for the next level.

CPSIA information can be obtained
at www.ICGtesting.com
Printed in the USA
LVHW082006200421
685033LV00002B/194

9 781647 024123